BETH BALL

AN AGE OF AZURIA
PREQUEL NOVELLA

Published by Grove Guardian Press

Edited by The Blue Garret

Cover design by Mibl Art

Ebook ISBN 978-1-952609-09-1

Paperback ISBN 978-1-952609-10-7

Hardback ISBN 978-1-952609-11-4

groveguardianpress.com

ALSO BY BETH BALL

Age of Azuria

Buried Heroes

Hadvarian Heist

Amber Queen

Forest Deep

Shadows Beneath (expected 2026)

Feather & Flame

Phoenix Rising

Heir of Lilith Trilogy

Phantom

Pain (forthcoming)

Novellas and Short Stories

Aurora, an *Age of Azuria* novella

Song of Parting, an *Age of Azuria* novella

Story Magic, an *Age of Azuria* novella

"Blood Wolf Moon" an *Age of Azuria* story

"The Shadow's Embrace" an *Age of Azuria* story

"Awakened Flame" an *Age of Azuria* story

"Nocturne" an *Age of Azuria* story

To Dermot and David
and the artists who came before

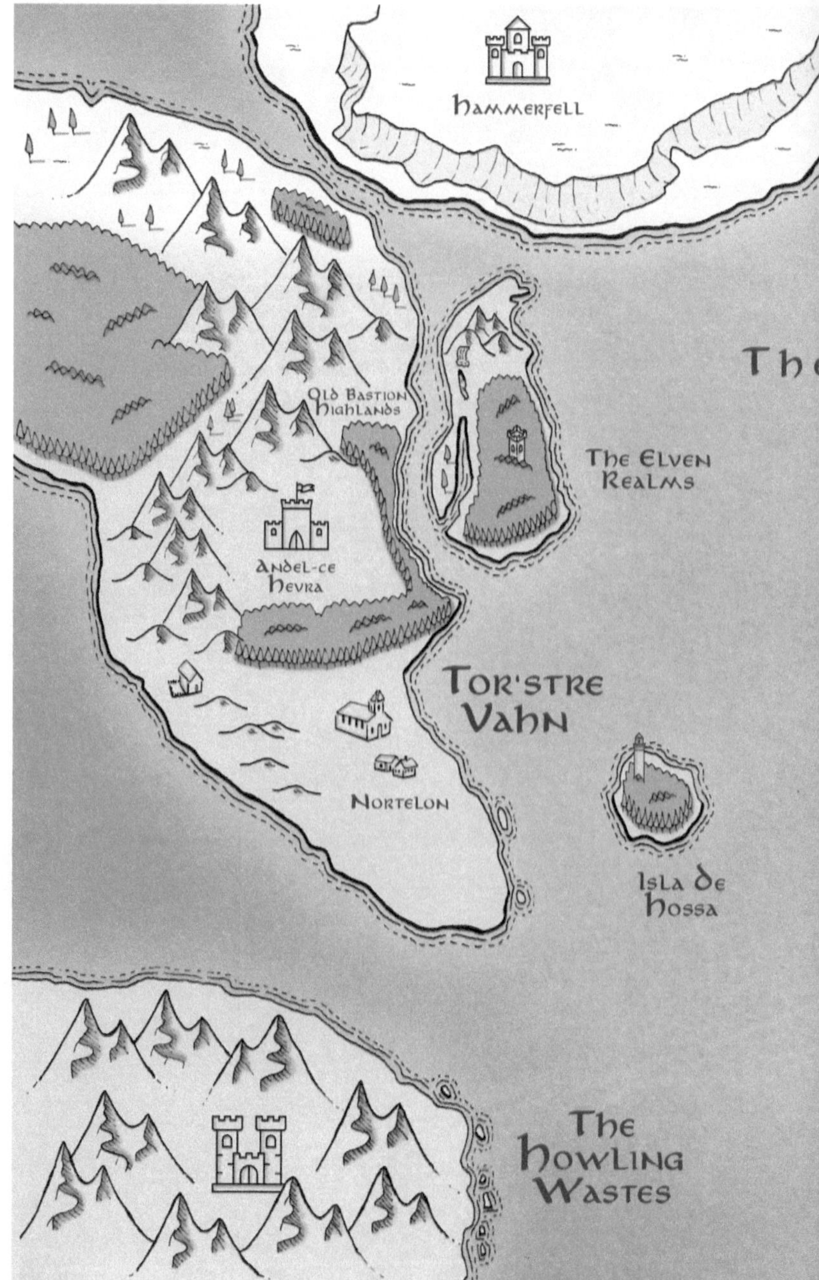

hammerfell
Old Bastion Highlands
The Elven Realms
Andel-ce Hevra
Tor'stre Vahn
Nortelon
Isla de hossa
The Howling Wastes
The

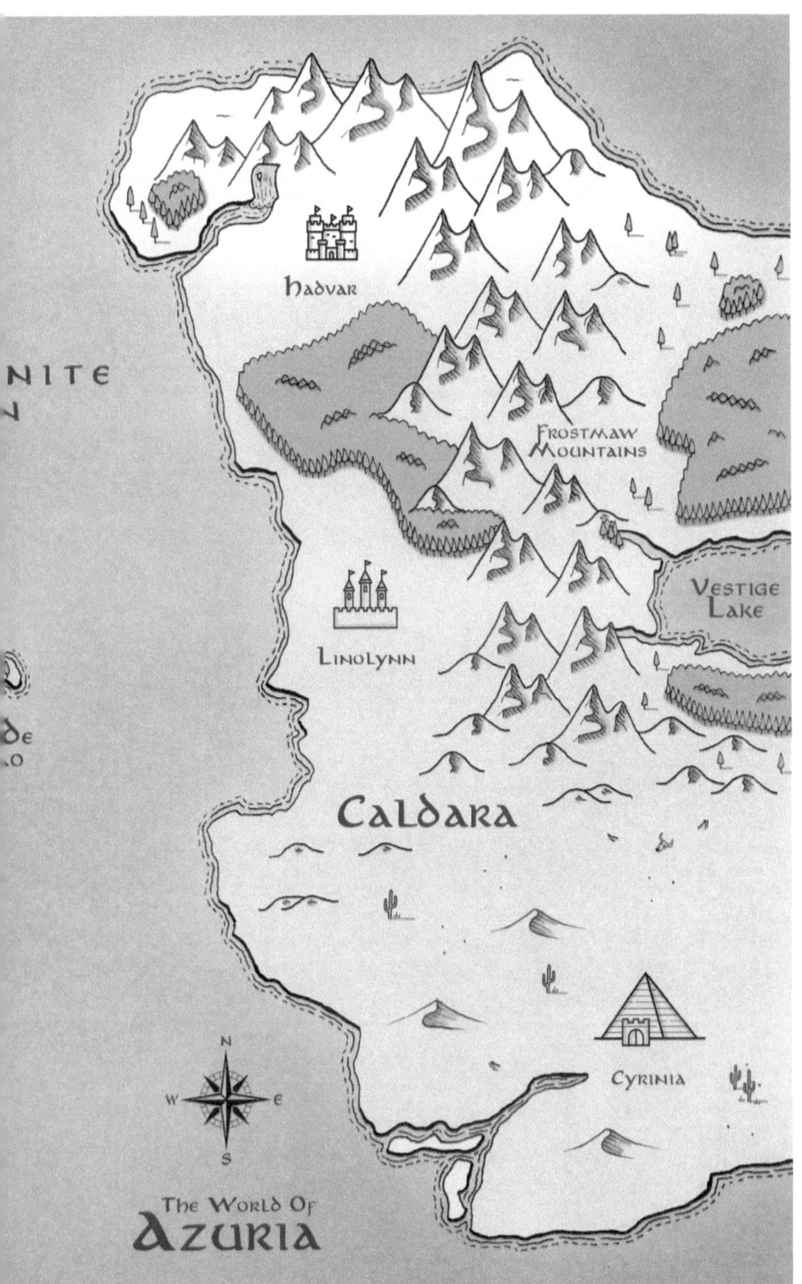
NITE
Hadvar
Frostmaw
Mountains
Vestige
Lake
Linolynn
Caldara
Cyrinia
N
W
E
S
The World Of
Azuria

CHAPTER 1

HUGH

Hugh leaned back against a tree, his eyes roving from left to right through the surrounding forest. The spirit had to be here somewhere. He sighed and rested the back of his head on the bark. If only he could blend into the forest as the spirits did. But he remained an outsider to these woods.

The spirit stirred again, sending ripples of energy darting around his feet through the layers of roots and fungi hidden beneath the cover of leaves and dirt. *More of the lycan are here among us. Watch them.*

He and his people never took more than their share, but the earth remained hesitant to welcome them, Fenrir's second people. "Lead them, help them adapt," the wolf god had said. Hugh was trying.

He pushed himself off the tree and followed after the spirit, rolling each step gently from heel to toe. *Snap.* He groaned as a twig cracked in two beneath his boot. Now any creature within the nearest acre would know where he was.

A blur of pale yellow sunlight rushed past him. He

spun to chase it. If the spirit was truly calling him . . . Hugh shook his head. Was this nothing more than wishful thinking to distract himself from the necessity of hunting in the fae woodland?

Thin beams of light filtered through the canopy ahead, creating rays of their own and lighting the world in a warm green glow. He continued, deeper into the wood than he'd yet ventured.

The green grew darker as the trees thickened, as though dusk had fallen early and he had entered a realm of twilight. The spirit pulsed up ahead, calling him.

"Why do you hunt in my wood?" A woman's voice dashed around the trees as though they spoke and not she.

Hugh froze, searching the forest for the speaker. "I—forgive me, lady. I did not know this was your wood." Not even a leaf moved in the trees around him. The forest held its breath.

A woman with pale golden skin slipped from behind one of the old oaks and stepped forward—her green longbow, covered in vines, was pulled taut, its arrow aimed at the center of his chest. "Did you not?" Dark red curls cascaded over her shoulder as she tilted her head. "Are you sure?"

The spirit that had haunted him throughout the morning, that had brought him deep into the forest, blew a cold breeze against his bare neck. The wolf in his heart howled in reply. He couldn't stay here. It was time to flee or attack. And yet his own spirit had grown roots. He could not move away.

"Tell me." Her bright green eyes flashed. A ripple of energy struck his chest.

"A spirit called to me. Guided me here."

The woman's face betrayed no emotion. Was she going to shoot him?

She stepped closer. Her golden skin glinted in the low forest light. "Is that so?"

"It is, lady." He bowed his head once and returned his gaze to hers.

"And why might it have called you, Hugh of the lycan?"

The question glimmered behind her eyes. Was she alone in this wood? Were her people nearby? "To find you, mistress of the dark wood."

The woman lowered her bow halfway and let slack the string. She studied him a moment longer, and her lips stretched into a smile. "Very well, Hugh of the lycan. We have met. What now?"

She was nothing like the women of his pack. Despite the straightforward air of her speech, hidden meanings flickered through the shadows behind her utterances. He chose his words carefully, not wishing to offend her or startle her into fleeing back into the depths of the wood. "The custom among my people would be for you to tell me your name, as you already know mine." Around them, the forest light dimmed, concentrating on the woman before him. Flecks of gold danced in her eyes and across her skin.

Still she watched him with amusement. "And if it is not the custom of mine to tell it? What then?"

Hugh allowed himself to smile. If she'd wanted to kill him, she would have already. "I shall have to uncover it or invent one myself for the time being."

She took another step and lowered the longbow to her side. A breeze picked up—the spirits' tide. The wind carried oak moss, cinnamon, and myrrh through his nostrils. "For the time being." She smiled again and disappeared into the thick copse behind her.

❦

KATARINA

Katarina Starsend lowered her long feather quill, sitting back in her chair with a smile. "That came out rather well, if I do say so myself."

The still-damp parchment grinned in reply.

Tales passed through the ages had always fascinated her, but *The Ballad of Hugh and Lilia* held a special place in her heart. It had been one of her mother's favorites, before her untimely passing, and was one of the first works she had set about independently translating in her early years as a scholar.

It had not been until her time with the gnomes, however, that her passion for the story was raised to new heights. A curious visitor to their collective, a friendly gnome by the name of Red, had told her of a fringe theory related to the famous couple. "There is evidence," he had explained, "of the two not only genuinely existing"—a suspicion Katarina had long held to be true—"but of their being *reborn*." The gnome's voice had squeaked, his eyes wide, as though the final word held a world of its own, a new paradigm around which to orient her life.

Which had been precisely what occurred.

Reading back through Red's trail of evidence, Katarina found many false rebirths alongside a few plausible reincarnations. At the gnome's invitation, she had taken up residence in a small cabin a day's ride from Red's Cross, on the edge of the Stormside Forest, and helped him tackle the question of how they might identify a true rebirth if one were to occur in their lifetime.

Wax dripped from her candle onto the curved tray of

its holder. She blew softly across the final shimmers of ink, waiting for the newest translation into Caldaran to dry.

Hooves clattered on the stone path outside her cabin. Katarina rose and ran to the door. Aravar, her older brother, was riding a great black stallion that cantered straight for her. Katarina ducked back inside the threshold door as he pulled the horse to a stop and swung down.

"Baby sister!" Aravar's white teeth gleamed against his dark skin. Katarina ran to meet him, and her brother swung her up into his arms. "Let me see." He pulled back and reached for her hands, turning them over. "Ah, here we are. Just as I suspected." Aravar pointed to the ink stains along her fingers from her quill and blotting paper. "You've been hard at work already today?"

Katarina brushed her braids back over her shoulder. "There are countless stories in the world, and they're in desperate need of recording." She grinned and took the reins of his horse, leading the stallion to the pen in the small orchard behind her cabin.

"I was hoping you would say that." Aravar's eyes flashed over the back of his horse as he began to remove the saddle. "I have something of note to share with you, actually."

Katarina's pulse quickened. "Have you really?"

"Yes, little sister." The brush bristles swished over the stallion's black coat. "Your special project, searching for the new incarnations of Lilia throughout history?"

She leaned in closer. Aravar's gaze followed a pair of sparrows flitting through of the eaves of the orchard. Katarina bounced back and forth from foot to foot. The stallion noticed her nervous energy and pawed the earth. "Just tell me. Did you find her?"

Another bright smile. "We may have. I followed Red's

notes, checking up on the various accounts he's collected." Katarina held her breath. They had been waiting for a chance like this in their research. "Kat, she's alive now. To the east, in the kingdom and court of Linolynn, a young half-elf."

Katarina narrowed her eyes, waiting for her brother to indicate he was less than serious.

His eyebrows contracted. "Did you hear me? We could go meet her, now!"

She skipped around to the other side of the horse and hugged Aravar. "Is it really true? What did Red say?"

Aravar grinned. "He wants you to go investigate, of course. Said he'd help connect you with the scholars there and would put you as close to her as possible. I have his letter of recommendation here somewhere . . ." He patted his pockets.

"You probably left it in the saddlebags." Aravar tended to misplace small items, especially when he was excited about a project.

"Ah, yes, right again." He shrugged and resumed brushing. "Anyway, I thought I would stop here, have a cup of tea with you, rest the horse, share the good news, and escort you to Io Keep."

"That sounds perfect." Katarina's arms wrapped around her waist, her mind spinning at the possibilities. "I can hardly believe it. All this morning, I've been working on translating one of the lesser-known versions of Hugh and Lilia's story. I just finished the account of their meeting if you'd like to read it while you rest."

Aravar patted the stallion's nose and led him over to a barrel of rainwater. After the horse had drank his fill, her brother strode toward the fence and sprang over the wooden railing. "I would love nothing more."

Katarina laughed and hurried after him, letting herself out of the gate. She withdrew Lilia's portion of the story from the stack of notes on her kitchen table. "Here you are—read away."

LILIA

Lilia grinned to herself as she departed. The lycan were as her mother had said, intriguing but easily captivated. She and her people hadn't much room to complain, being recent arrivals from the Brightlands themselves. But their seers had foretold of a curse—of heartbreak, betrayal, and separation—brought about by the lycan. She'd needed to find out more on her own.

"Where were you this morning, child?" Enid's voice encircled her daughter and pulled her closer.

Lilia met her eyes. "You know very well, Mother."

"Was your curiosity satisfied?"

"You know that also."

Her mother laughed. "What I truly knew was that I was going to have trouble from you. I should have made you from a different part of myself, but I could not bear it."

Lilia shook her head. The fae queen had formed her from a collection of spring twigs, leaves, and grasses, and over a period of thirty days, poured some of her life energy into them. Her mother was fond of taking credit for Lilia's idiosyncrasies, her endless questions about the ways of life so quickly accepted by the rest of their people.

"Come, daughter"—Enid reached out for her hand— "the Council would speak with us."

"Yes, Reya." Lilia walked beside her mother over the moss-covered stones, cool and wet against her bare feet. Their people stopped as their queen and her daughter passed, bowing their heads outside their tree hollows or pausing along the sweeping vine passageways above. Enid smiled and acknowledged each of them. She was much beloved by their people. Lilia, less so.

She couldn't shake her astonishment at her encounter with the lycan. He had seemed so startled by her. Was he truly unaware of their home in the heart of the forest?

Mottled sunlight shone down into the meeting grove, and Enid released her daughter's hand to speak with the seers. They bowed to their queen, the dark tips of their leafy robes caressing their dried leafy cousins on the forest floor.

The younger seers gathered beside the sacred stream that trickled through the clearing, and the rest of the fae followed behind their queen and spread slowly around the verdant circle. Dryads leaned out of their tree trunks to follow the proceedings. Eravenor, Lilia's white antlered doe, poked her head through the greenery, and she hurried to her side.

"Shh," Lilia cooed as she stroked the creature's nose, "are you supposed to be here?"

The doe's eyes widened, asking her friend and mistress the same question. "Mother insisted, I swear. We've all gathered." Lilia laid her forehead against her companion's and then watched as her flower-clad antlers and frost-white rump disappeared into the Darkwood's embrace.

"Ewan'il smiles upon you, Reyanna," a smooth tenor voice rumbled softly behind her.

Lilia turned. Dagnan, the youngest council member, watched her.

"And why might you think that?"

"The hunter guardian sends one of his prize spirit creatures, a sign of goodness, fortune, and prosperity to your side. At such a time as this, it bodes well."

"Such a time as what, Del Dagnan?"

"Come sit next to your mother and you shall see." He smiled and extended his hand. Lilia's gold fingers slid over his evergreen palm, his skin the texture of a sun-warmed stone lifted from the riverbank. He held her hand in both of his and walked backward to the edge of the circle, depositing her beside her mother.

Enid lifted an eyebrow in surprise, but Lilia shook her head. She and her mother both knew Dagnan did not intend the gesture as a sign of intention to the rest of the community. His primary objective remained influence over the fae, but wooing the reyanna would not help his quest for increased power.

Dagnan bowed to his fellow council members and took his seat along the low-hanging branch of the terra tree.

Criane, the Elder, rose to speak. "My friends, we come together at this urgent time. While the sun finds her peak above us, darkness gathers beyond our horizons. Though it is not the darkness we had feared." The eldest seer paused as a collective wave of surprise crested over the gathering. "Beyond our own plane, across the heavens and below, ill intent gathers. The brewing storm will spell the end."

Muffled cries rang out across the circle.

"Speak plainly!"

"What does she mean?"

"What have you seen?"

Criane raised her hands for silence. "Our people, change is upon us, whether we would seek it or not. This world will be the battleground, across the ages. As the fae who have walked upon this new earth, we must decide where we stand."

Lilia's eyes bounded over the gathering of her people. The sparks of unease in her chest and stomach burned in the eyes of those around her. What was this growing darkness? The fae did not fear the day or the night—they were simply reflections of one another. The ill intent Criane spoke of mattered more.

Her mother's mouth pressed in a tight line, but she did not seem as distressed or surprised at this news as the rest of the community. The queen had seen something. Their eyes met. "I have been asking you to prepare, have I not?" she whispered.

"Yes, you have, Mother, but why?"

The queen laid her hand on Lilia's shoulder. "You will soon see."

CHAPTER 2

TEODRIC

Hazy rays of autumn light trickled through panes of glass. Outside Teodric's window, low gray clouds hung heavy over the ocean, and mist slithered across Linolynn's docks, dampening the sounds of their early morning bustle. The young nobleman strummed absent-mindedly at his lute, his thoughts drifting away on the currents of the melody.

Knuckles rapped gently against the wooden frame of his door.

"Come in," Teodric called.

The hinge creaked as his father pushed the door open. Frederick Adhemar creased his thick brown eyebrows as he stared at him. He looked down at his hands, wringing them together.

"Father, what is it? Are you unwell?" Teodric set his lute to the side and rose from the low couch. "Is it Mother?"

"No, no, I am perfectly well." Frederick shook his head. "And your mother is fine, do not worry."

"What is it then?" His father had to have come in for something.

"Let's you and I take a stroll around the conservatory."

They walked side by side through the castle's guest wing and down to the main level. The gardens spanned the western side of the grounds, looking out over the ocean along the edge of the wall. Frederick led him into the glass enclosure of one of the greenhouses, the heady aroma of herbs and fruits flooding his senses.

"Before I speak, you must promise to keep what I have to tell you in confidence."

"Father, I shall, but—"

"It's about Iellieth."

A rush of cold jolted up Teodric's spine. "What about her?"

Frederick sighed. His leather soles scraped against the rocky dirt path that wound between the flowerbeds as he passed the small citrus trees in their planters. He stopped at the edge of the hexagonal boundary that surrounded the flowers and the elaborate fountain in the center of the greenhouse.

Teodric ground his teeth, following close behind. Why was he hesitating? What could have happened?

His father leaned his forearms against the iron railing, and Teodric followed suit. The painted metal pressed a cold kiss against his sleeve, penetrating through to his skin.

"You know that your mother and I have spoken to Duchess Amastacia in the past about her . . . intentions for her daughter."

Teodric's jaw twitched. It wasn't her mother's intentions that would determine Iellieth's fate. The duke's dark shadow loomed in the corner of his mind.

"It seems that they are moving their plans forward and will be bringing suitors to the castle sooner than anticipated."

A knot formed in Teodric's throat. He clutched his hands together, the knuckles whitening against his skin.

Frederick spoke softly into the silence as Teodric fought to regain his composure. "I know that you have suspected as much, understanding her family as you do."

Hot tears prickled against Teodric's eyes. If he could swallow this knot, he could set his father's mind at ease. The bind only thickened in his throat.

"Your mother and I wanted to say something sooner. But it seemed cruel to dampen your time together with worries for the future. We thought they might wait until she was older—"

"I knew, Father." He couldn't abide the pain in Frederick's voice any longer. It threatened to overwhelm his own, which raged already, a storm he could scarcely control.

Lord Adhemar nodded. "I suspected as much." He turned to Teodric and wrapped his son's cold, tanned hands in his own warm grasp. "But I am afraid I must ask one more thing of you."

Teodric's brow furrowed. He cleared his throat. "What is it, Father?"

"You must promise me to tell her nothing about it."

His head jerked to the side to meet his father's gaze. Dark brown irises ringed in a bronze halo stared back at him, pleading. "Why?" The word burned as he spoke.

Frederick pulled his lips in together, his mustache bristling. "For the same reason I have said nothing to you before now. We've no cause to worry her in advance. You can protect her freedom."

"Her illusion of freedom." Teodric pulled away from his father's grasp and strode toward the exit.

"Would you take that from her as well?" Frederick called after him.

Teodric stopped. His shoulders fell. Had he a choice in the matter? "No, Father, you are right. I won't tell her."

A small, sad smile flickered across his father's face. "I am sorry, son. And I'm proud of you."

Teodric bowed his head and turned to go, leaving Frederick by the fountain.

He paced the castle halls. Keeping his promise to his father didn't mean that he couldn't start planning a way for Iellieth to keep her freedom—true freedom, not an illusion—and to help her find a way out of her stepfather the duke's plot.

❧

Iellieth's green eyes sparkled in the dim corridor overlooking the castle courtyard. She leaned toward him, her breath tickling his ear. "Teodric, what do you think of our new arrivals?"

Her rose-scented perfume rippled toward him, temporarily dulling his voice. He couldn't tell her the truth, regardless. *I hate them, as they've arrived to take you away from your home, away from me.* He'd promised Father, and himself, not to tell her unless they had no other option.

"Teodric?" She frowned up at him.

He rubbed the back of his neck. He knew he was behaving peculiarly, and he didn't trust himself to deliver a convincing lie. "Yes, sorry, they seem . . ." He squinted down from their hidden balcony. A human man in his early thirties stepped out of the coach and donned a blue hat with a large, floppy feather. "Should we say fond of birds, or does such an accessory display a hatred for the creatures?" If he couldn't affect a lighter tone, he would need to spend the afternoon apart from her. She'd grow too suspicious otherwise. How often in the few weeks since Father had warned him had he questioned whether or not she already knew?

Iellieth giggled watching the feathered hat bounce with each of the man's prancing steps. "I suppose it depends on how willingly we believe the bird sacrificed its feather for the hat." Her expression fell as she studied him more closely. "Are you truly dreading the ball tomorrow this much? Who has your mother picked out for you to escort?"

Close, very close. "Oh, I can't remember." Teodric shrugged and turned back to the window. "I believe her name starts with an *R*?" He glanced over to Scad for a distraction while he gathered himself. Their young friend had enough enthusiasm for the three of them to share.

"Are we waiting for them to *do* something?" Scad pressed his forehead against the window, leaving a smudge. "Why don't they ever travel with anyone interesting?"

Teodric chuckled. Scad never failed him.

The young servant boy scowled at the new arrivals. "I thought there might be knights this time at least. Or some sort of hunt or festival."

"Whatever gave you that idea?" Iellieth peered at her friend before returning her attention outside.

"I just keep hoping something exciting will happen around here, that's all." Scad drew himself up to full height and scrunched one side of his face. "Lady Amastacia"—he lowered his voice a full octave—"shall we adjourn?" He waved his arm in a series of circles before narrowing the flourish enough for Iellieth to grab on to his elbow.

She shook her head, smiling. "You're only cranky because you're hungry." Iellieth tucked an errant strand of long garnet hair behind her ear, pivoting in the narrow passageway to address him. "I believe we are in need of a trip to the kitchens, Lord Adhemar." Iellieth followed Scad's example and spoke in her most noble, breathy tones. She grabbed his hand and pulled him along after her and Scad down the wood-paneled passageway.

Teodric's heart swelled against his ribs. Her laughter shone all around him, and he alone could perceive the clouds on the horizon. What if they never had another opportunity to sneak around the castle precisely like this? Why was Duke Amastacia determined to send her away?

CHAPTER 3

IELLIETH

Iellieth groaned and stomped back into her room. It was absurd to demand that she cancel her entire afternoon to get ready for a ball that evening.

"We are honored you could fit us into your schedule, Henri." Mamaun's voice swooped down the hall, pecking at her with the supposed importance of the castle's designer arriving to attend particularly to the fit of her gown.

It took both Henri and Bridget, their ladies' maid, to get Iellieth into the dress. "It's too tight." She scowled at Mamaun, who shook her head. Behind the duchess, an afternoon's worth of reading pouted by the window, the abandoned stories staring out at the sea.

"You look gorgeous, dear," Henri said, her thick Caldaran accent meant to soothe the irritated puff of Iellieth's internal feathers.

Two thin, useless straps hung off her shoulders, and the dress clung to her every curve, stopping a few inches beneath her knees. The cerulean fabric had a delicate aqua sheen that accentuated the green of Iellieth's eyes, especially after the designer applied small, glittering stars across one shoulder, with a few more sprinkled on her cheeks, eyelashes, and hair. "It's lovely, Henri." She grinned politely. It wasn't Henri's fault her afternoon translations had been postponed. "But how am I supposed to dance in it? Mamaun, you said that it's important for me to be dancing tonight, yes?" She wriggled to show the gown's constricting design. Perhaps whatever reason had sparked this unusual interest in her preparations would overrule the binding gown.

"You'll get along fine." Mamaun rose from the chair to help Bridget adjust Iellieth's hair. "I'm sure it will loosen somewhat as the evening goes on, isn't that right, Henri?"

"Certainly, Your Grace." Henri's smile flashed bright beneath her blue lips. Iellieth crossed her arms. She would have felt better borrowing the designer's lipstick and pretending to be a mermaid or attending a costume party like they sometimes held in Hadvar. But why make such a fuss when they weren't even leaving the castle?

Mamaun stepped back to evaluate their hard work. "Bridget, go with Henri to find a pair of shoes for my daughter to wear tonight. Henri"—she returned the designer's wide smile—"we are truly in your debt. Thank you." The other two women curtsied before hurrying out of the room.

Iellieth bit the inside of her lip watching them go. Mamaun had something on her mind that she didn't want anyone else to hear.

"Now, Iellieth, I want you to pay careful attention to Lord Glenwood tonight. He's traveled quite far to visit us here, and he is most anxious to meet you. I expect you to dance with him as often as you're able and to ensure he's watching when you're with someone else."

Iellieth stared back at her mother. She must be referring to the man they'd seen with the feathered hat. If she started with the most obvious questions first, she would work her way toward her mother's odd behavior around the evening. "How am I supposed to control what he's looking at, especially when we're on opposite sides of a room?"

Mamaun threw her head back and groaned. "Don't be on the opposite side of the room, then."

Her mother wasn't making sense. "We haven't ever met before. Why has he already decided to pay particular attention to me?" *Why is this so important to you?* she longed to ask.

"Stop being ridiculous."

Iellieth pulled away from Mamaun's tone.

Her mother sighed and laid her hands flat against the base of her ribs, frowning at the ceiling. Her upper lip remained pursed as she spoke, her tone flatter but reserved. "The duke will introduce the two of you this evening, and he will be your escort for the gala. Now, you must excuse me"—her mother swept her skirt to the side and glided toward the door—"I must away to prepare for this evening myself."

She watched her mother's retreating form. There had never been this much insistence and control over her behavior at one of the palace gatherings before.

Henri appeared at the door. Iellieth waved her in. The designer knelt on the floor and helped Iellieth slide her feet into a pair of silver heels constructed from straps of leather. Henri looked up at her sadly and patted her calf. "We'll figure out something that better suits you for the next one, sweetheart."

"Henri . . ." Perhaps the designer knew something she didn't. "What did my mother—"

She rose, shaking her head. "I really must be going, miss." Henri squeezed her hand. "You'll be fine. Try not to worry."

The pieces started to float together in the back of Iellieth's mind, but she turned away from the picture they showed her. That couldn't be it.

"I'll ask Bridget to come fetch you when it's time."

Iellieth nodded, silent as Henri left the room.

The books on her desk shook their heads. Even they knew. She drifted over to join them, slumped into her desk chair, and laid her forehead against her arms.

❦

TWO HOURS LATER, IELLIETH PROCEEDED WITH HER family down to the receiving hall and the ballrooms that abutted the gardens. The plants glistened beyond the glittering walls, offering fresh air and sanctuary for those who abandoned one form of liveliness for another.

She would feel better when Teodric arrived. Iellieth clutched her arms, trying to rid her palms of their cold sweat. At any moment, her unknown escort was supposed to appear.

The duke had glowered when she emerged from her room, regarding her, as usual, like she emanated an unpleasant odor. "I suppose that will do," he said to Mamaun before whirling his attention back to her. "Stop sulking." His sallow skin stretched from grimace to grin as he took her mother's arm and led them down to the ballroom. Bruden, her half-brother, clumped behind her down the halls. They had nothing to say to one another while his sister Lucinda—her half-sister—was away.

Iellieth closed her eyes against the glow all around her and imagined floating out beyond the garden doors. A few at the opposite end of the hall had been flung open, inviting the sea breeze to join in their feast and festivities, but all the nobility would stay inside for the first several hours.

She clung to the vision of moonlight rippling over the ocean waves for a final moment, her fingers wrapped around her father's amulet. The duke's guest had arrived.

Her stepfather's oily voice interrupted her reverie. "Lord Benedict Glenwood, of course, such a pleasure." The duke's thin lips stretched into a tight smile as he introduced the nobleman from the other side of the Frostmaw Mountains to his wife and son. "And please allow me to introduce"—his hand swept toward Iellieth— "my stepdaughter, Lady Iellieth Amastacia."

Iellieth curtsied and raised her eyes to her escort. A man in his mid-thirties, twice her age, stared back at her. He had a kind smile, though no clever lights danced in his dark blue eyes. "Beautiful Lady Amastacia"—he bowed— "might I take you for a turn across the floor?"

"Yes, you may." She accepted his proffered glove. The duke's cold stare followed her around the room. That, at least, was the same as always.

Lord Glenwood spoke of his journey around Vestige Lake and the lovely autumn forests he'd traversed on his way west to Linolynn. She had so many questions—it was rare that she encountered someone who had traveled far beyond the castle walls, and so recently. Was this why Mamaun had wanted them to meet?

The novelty wore off quickly. They hadn't stopped very

often, he explained, as the party had been late setting out. "And there is only so much to say about trees." He winked at this, and Iellieth's heart sank lower in her chest. One day, she would find out for herself. Somehow. She sighed and turned back to the ballroom.

Teodric and his family had just entered the room on the opposite end. He was escorting a tall and pretty brunette this evening, a young woman she hadn't seen before. His mother spoke excitedly to Teodric's partner, who smiled and laughed at Lady Adhemar's remarks, the perfect picture of how one should perform at a gala. Iellieth chewed on her bottom lip as the evening's dull shadow stretched out before her.

Lord Glenwood swept her out onto the floor as she tried unsuccessfully to catch Teodric's eye. "I want to assure you, Lady Amastacia," Lord Glenwood's voice called her attention back to him, "that I have many ambitious plans for the future, assuming they are agreeable to you, of course."

She blinked back at him. "Pardon me, what did you say?"

"In the mountains," he added cryptically. Had he returned to the subject of his journey here? "There will need to be a larger home, of course, and expanded trade routes along the range. I believe it would benefit your family as well. We'll be careful with which estates have the most advantageous routes, eh?"

"Routes to where?" She felt breathless. The sparkly dress was clutching her too tightly, that was all.

"To the usual trading hubs, of course, though I hear you're fond of the sea, and I'm sure we can figure something out if you insist. I am hoping that a lake might do just as well. It's so much nearer. Would you terribly mind the compromise?"

Her stomach burbled up into her throat, rising in waves that pulled the breath from her lungs. Lord Glenwood was speaking of a match between the two of them, an estate for them to share. The edges of the ballroom spun. Had her family already engaged her to this man who spoke of little beyond commerce and routes? Who had the luxury of travel and failed to notice the intricate details of the trees or the unique sense of disparate landscapes?

Iellieth laid a cold hand against her neck, but it did little to soothe her whirling thoughts or strangled breath.

If only Scad had sneaked in, or if she could find Teodric nearby. Katarina, her tutor and friend, had already disappeared back to her rooms for the evening, her elegant partner following close behind.

She clawed at the gathering fog, pushing back against the grasping tide that would pull her under. Spiraling tendrils of pure ice spread along the base of her throat. Iellieth locked eyes with the duke.

He watched her and Lord Glenwood with a smirk as he twirled his middle finger over the rim of his glass, tracing the golden ring around and around again. His eyes glinted as he saw her finally put all the disparate pieces together— the special evening, the gown, her mother's particular instructions. Lord Glenwood was only the first, a test. A long line of ghostly suitors spread out before her, each with her stepfather's thin sickle grin.

Iellieth turned back to the suitor, her eyes glassy. The nearest of the specters superimposed its visage over his. Her knees gave way beneath her.

CHAPTER 4

TEODRIC

Teodric leapt over and caught Iellieth around the waist, pulling her from her suitor's weak grasp. The distress contorting her face fell away as she slumped against his shoulder. "Let me take you outside," Teodric whispered. With a tiny nod, she nestled deeper into his chest.

"Lord Glenwood, if you would be so kind as to fetch the lady a glass of water and meet us in the garden."

"I . . . yes, I shall." The alarmed nobleman nodded and skidded off to do as Teodric wished.

He would save his ire for the duke for another time.

Teodric kept a tight hold of Iellieth as he angled them toward the open doors, trying to excite as little fuss as possible. Luckily, she had been near the edge of the ballroom already, the lull of the ocean calling her out and away. Only a few nearby had seen what happened. He smiled to them and nodded as he walked her outside. These things happened at galas now and then.

Especially when the duke was staring at someone as he

had been at Iellieth. Had anyone else besides him witnessed their wordless exchange?

Iellieth looked up, bright green eyes wide with panic. Her breath was too shallow and came and left too quickly. "Shh, you're alright. Trust me," he urged.

Teodric had kept a close eye on Iellieth since the moment he and Rosa arrived. His partner was charming, as most of his mother's selections for him were, but he had been distracted immediately by his father's warning coming true before him.

His breath caught at the sight of Iellieth in her blue-green dress, the shimmer it threw over her skin. A cruel voice sneered in the back of his mind—she had been forced to wear it for *her* escort for the evening, so any benefit was for *him* and him alone. A man named Lord Glenwood, apparently, with overly trimmed facial hair who attempted, poorly, to match her graceful steps across the ballroom.

Night had fully descended around them. Colorful lanterns, designed to look like faery lights, hung from leaf-laden branches in the trees. Teodric guided her to the side of the garden, far enough to be hidden from easy view of the ballroom but not so far that Lord Glenwood would raise an alarm when he couldn't find her.

When she managed to take in the sights around them, she would see one of her favorite trees in all of the gardens, an ancient oak, presiding calmly over her companions, a few thin willows dancing around her feet.

Iellieth's breathing slowed. A tear glinted on her cheek. He caught it before it dashed against the starry glitter.

Lord Glenwood hurried toward them with two glasses, some of the contents of which he had spilled on himself in his haste. Teodric smiled, this small error raising the man in his esteem. The foreign nobleman wasn't the one who was to blame.

"Iellieth," he said softly, waiting for her eyes to stop their frantic survey of her surroundings and focus on his, "we've got you some water. You're going to be fine. Nothing else is going to happen."

The visiting lord's hand shook as he handed Iellieth her glass. She took the cup with both hands and rested it against her bottom lip, peering out over the rim. Lord Glenwood took a deep swig from the glass in his other hand and then held it out to Teodric. The liquid was pale amber instead of clear—a glass of watered-down spirits. He likewise took a gulp of the chilled whiskey, winced appreciatively, and handed it back to the visiting noble-man. "That's pretty good." The earthiness with a hint of smoke brought back crisp autumn mornings on his family's estate in the foothills.

"We brought a few casks with us over the Frostmaws as a gift. I'm relieved they went ahead and opened them." He walked around their position at the base of a tree and squatted down in front of Iellieth to be eye level with her. "I'll leave the two of you here for a spell, shall I?" Glen-wood glanced at him. "There's a kind woman with long brown hair looking for her escort inside. I'll dash off and assist her." He rapped his knuckles against the trunk. Bright yellow leaves fluttered to the ground. "Oh, and I'll send a servant out with fresh drinks as well."

Iellieth stared out across the gardens, looking through and beyond her suitor with no sign that she was aware of his presence before her.

"We would be most obliged, Lord Glenwood, thank you." Teodric nodded to the man with a small smile.

A breeze trickled through the branches of the Arboretum, and the garden flowers swayed. "Thank you," Iellieth whispered over her water glass.

"My pleasure." Glenwood bowed and strode back into the hall.

Iellieth set her cup down and laid her head against his shoulder. "You knew, didn't you?"

He couldn't lie to her about that now, but how could he help her to understand? "Yes." Teodric held his breath. Would she be as angry with him as she undoubtedly was with the duke?

She rolled her head back, angling her eyes up to his. "What are we going to do?"

Teodric turned, her hair tickling his nose and lips. He wanted to kiss the top of her head but thought better of it. "Well, first, I think we should try to hear the ocean over the twentieth waltz of the night. And then maybe you and I can take a walk around these trees?"

"That sounds lovely." Iellieth scooted in closer to him and closed her eyes.

Waves crashed along Linolynn's rocky shore, punctuating the viols' melody. The day his father told him about the suitors, he had begun working on a song for Iellieth. The words for the verses came slowly, and then the chorus, but the notes eluded him.

Beneath the crescendo of the waves, the leaves picked up their song, carrying the music across the gardens. The trees sang his melody, the key changing from minor to major. Swaying branches wafted the transition chords gently into his mind.

CHAPTER 5

IELLIETH

Lord Glenwood stayed for breakfast the next morning. He spoke kindly to Iellieth but paid most of his attention to Duke Amastacia and her half-brother, Bruden.

Mamaun dabbed at her lips with her napkin and laid it gently across the table. "Iellieth, why don't you take Lord Glenwood on a tour of the Keep this morning? The first of the leaves in the Arboretum have begun to change, and he had little time to view the castle yesterday."

Glenwood lurched forward, nearly upsetting his individual serving of jam in his haste. "My most gracious hostess, I am afraid I must beg your forgiveness for what I am about to say. An urgent matter came to my attention this morning. My steward is busy preparing our coaches, and we must away. I only told him that first, I needed a chance to speak with my generous hosts, for I could not part from here otherwise."

Mamaun sat back in her chair, eyes narrowed. Iellieth's suitor took advantage of the moment's pause and turned to her. He reached out for her hand and clasped it between each of his own. "Beautiful Lady Amastacia, I beg that you find it in your heart to forgive me. Truly, parting from you grieves me more than I can say."

Iellieth had witnessed the sincere passion in Lord Glenwood's voice the night before as he talked about his estate and plans for the future. His earnest language was less flowery, more self-assured than these overeager entreaties. Her stepfather's eyes burned against the back of her neck from the head of the table, a stare that had to be visible to Glenwood as well. Was the nobleman trying to shift the blame from her to himself before making his exit?

She laid her free hand against her heart for her role in the performance. "Lord Glenwood, my mother and I are saddened greatly that you must leave us, though, of course, I hope all is well at your home."

"You are most kind, Lady Amastacia." He bowed his head over her hand. "Forgive me, all, I must be going."

Dappled autumn sunlight created a warm aura around her mother, whose posture had recovered during this exchange. "Calderon, perhaps you might accompany Lord Glenwood to the guest quarters to ensure they have everything they need for their journey?"

Cold sweat condensed against Iellieth's palms. With additional time alone together, the duke could try to convince Lord Glenwood to change his mind and stay. How could she strengthen his resolve? Her suitor had risen, and a small smirk played out across his face as he patted the back of her hand.

The duke continued to glare, but no matter how frosty his gaze, he could not force her to meet his eyes. She thought instead of the brilliance of the autumn leaves in the weeks ahead, the fiery scarlets and oranges accented by topaz, merlot, and the deep shades of the evergreens.

"Send Merud down to me as soon as may be," the duke snapped. He bowed his head to Lord Glenwood and marched after him down the hall.

Iellieth shivered. Was her stepfather's steward meant to help the visitors in their departure or to call up the next in a prepared list of suitors? Muffled voices echoed down the hall, but she couldn't make out their conversation.

Mamaun's sapphire eyes turned to her. "I want you to know—"

"I am actually running late to meet Katarina, Mamaun. Perhaps you'll excuse me, and you and the duke can scold me later today?" She sprang up from her chair and hurried from the breakfast room. Iellieth pressed her shaking hands against her abdomen. Any longer, and they would have sensed how much the evening before had upset her, more than they'd already seen from her fainting spell in the ballroom. She couldn't allow the duke that power over her.

Iellieth's heels clicked against the wooden floorboards as she rushed to the sanctuary of her room. The sun-bleached wood of her door beckoned, the portal to a place of light, literature, and the sounds of the sea. If only she could open the door and leap into one of the faery realms she so loved to read about—worlds of magic, wonder, and adventure instead of stuffy suitors and conniving step-fathers.

A figure on her reading chair sprang up as she entered, and Iellieth jumped back. "Scad, I didn't realize you—"

"Ellie, Teodric told me everything. What should we do? Where's Greenwood?" He ran toward the door as though the suitor might be waiting just on the other side of it.

She caught his arm as he darted past. "Shh, not here." Iellieth laid her finger against her lips, and Scad hunched down, gangly limbs forming sharp angles as he tried to compress his recently elongated frame. Her supplies for the morning's work rested on the desk next to the novel she'd begun reading to help herself calm down the night before. Scad followed her over to the semicircle of windows, asking questions and inventing his own redundant names for Lord Glenwood. She smiled. Each new name was as ill-fitting as the last for a man who cared nothing for forests and their ancient inhabitants. He finally paused for breath at Daleforest, and Iellieth interrupted him. "Lord Glenwood is leaving this morning, so you don't need to be worried." Her stomach twisted at lying to him—there would be cause enough for concern in the days ahead. But until she better understood the scope of her stepfather's plans, there was no need for Scad to upset himself when she was out of immediate danger.

Her friend scowled, confused. "Did he not like you? How is that—"

Iellieth laughed and guided Scad toward the servants' door in the wall. "I'll explain everything later, I promise."

He scurried out the door hidden in the wainscoting, and Iellieth returned to gathering her ink and parchment for her morning with Katarina. She loved delving into the lush language of a text in Celestial or Elvish and emerging from their depths with new iterations in Caldaran, to be read by a new audience and embedded in the stones of time. Katarina liked to say they were "contributing to history," an idea that made her chest swell with pride.

CHAPTER 6

KATARINA

atarina looked up from her parchment as hurried footsteps clacked toward her.

"I'm sorry I'm late," Iellieth whispered, sliding into the seat across from her at the wide wooden table. The girl's hair had retained most of its shape from the gala the night before, though her eyes were red-rimmed and puffy.

"Is everything alright?" Katarina reached across her assortment of pages for Iellieth's hand. Her skin was cold in spite of the library's blazing hearths.

"Not exactly." Iellieth looked down at her stack of books and ink.

After a few heartbeats passed, Katarina prodded again. "Did something happen last night?" Her curiosity upon first meeting the young half-elf had transformed into genuine affection. She couldn't yet conclusively say if Iellieth was a reborn Lilia, though the amulet she wore carried striking similarities to one held dear by a past incarnation, an elf named Rowan. But Katarina cared deeply for the girl regardless.

She listened without speech or surprise as Iellieth recounted her discovery of her stepfather's plans for her future, of Teodric coming to her aid. From what she'd observed, such arranged matches were less common in the Linolynnian court, but not so unheard of that Duke Amastacia's maneuvers would raise suspicion or concern outside of Iellieth's small circle of friends.

Her inner storyteller, the part of her that delighted in Hugh and Lilia's tales, in the process of discovery, wanted to assure Iellieth that, though the path seemed dark and impossible at the moment, she would find a way forward. But her own experience had taught her that such starry-eyed beliefs were not the only writers of history. Formidable, malignant forces also held sway, as Hugh and Lilia had found.

She finally settled on a compromise within herself, turning them both back to the reverie of their work. "Shall we see if the word-weavings of our translations whisk us away from present concerns?"

Iellieth pressed a fingertip to the corners of her eyelids and gave her a small smile. "Yes, I think that will help."

They set to work on a new sheaf of pages Aravar had uncovered, a rather dull history from the years after the great flood. Iellieth's quill moved slowly, and her eyes kept drifting to the windows. Perhaps it was time to share parts of Lilia's story with Iellieth. "Hmm, let's take a change of pace for the morning," Katarina said. "Why don't we sit by the fire and read, and we can resume our translations tomorrow?"

Iellieth grinned. "I would really like that." Her shoulders relaxed. "Can I read some of the story you've been working on?"

The pair of them resettled by one of the large fireplaces interspersed along the walls of the Librarium. Crisp leaves rustled outside the sweeping windows, waving crimson and orange hands at those nestled inside. Iellieth curled up in one of the plush leather armchairs with a small bundle of Katarina's translations, and she sat at the table beside the half-elf with a book of faery tales bound in dark olive green with gilt-edged pages.

Iellieth quickly disappeared into the story, the world of the past swirling around her, tugging her back into its embrace.

Katarina smiled. If she could choose a reborn Lilia, it would be the young woman sitting before her. And what better way for a new Lilia to equip herself for her own story than to know and learn from how her adventure had unfurled before?

HUGH

Hugh jerked his bow aside at the last moment, and the arrow flew far afield, narrowly missing the doe's flank. It had appeared almost by magic, one of Ewan'il's messengers, a white antlered doe blessed by the forest spirit.

The great creature watched him with its left eye, daring him to come closer. Hugh slung his longbow across his back and held out his hands as he crept forward. The doe had to know he meant it no harm.

"It was only an antlered hare," he soothed, his voice low. He'd been pursuing the smaller creature when the doe appeared before him. "Nothing like you, save its head attire. They're mean little brutes." The doe continued to watch him as he inched closer.

"Why've you come to me, eh? Are you hurt?" The creature stood erect, an ivory blaze in the deeply shaded forest. A tinge of hope lightened his voice. "Do you want to show me something?"

The doe darted away into the trees, and Hugh cursed. He'd be a fool not to follow it. Two days in a row he was chasing after spirits in the wood.

Each time he was sure he'd lost the trail or that the doe was beyond him, a rustle in the trees or flash of white appeared to spur him on. There, at the top of a ridge, its silhouette darted behind an ancient oak tree. Hugh picked up his pace. Surely he was getting close now.

Whap.

A gnarled branch flew out from behind the oak and struck his forehead. Hugh cried out in alarm and stumbled back. He fell, hard, against the leaf-padded ground, and a root bruised his hip for good measure.

A two-legged silhouette bearing antlers stood poised above him. Hugh scrambled back and called upon the wolf inside him, ready to make his escape.

Clouds shifted overhead, and light returned to the forest. The golden woman from the day before planted the end of her quarterstaff, the branch that had struck him, in the earth beside her.

"Are you hunting my companion?" She raised an auburn eyebrow, studying him.

Hugh rubbed his head. As he'd suspected, his hand came away sticky with blood. "I wasn't. The doe found me." He pushed himself up onto his elbows to get a better look at the fae woman who was staring down at him, amused by his plight. "Did you send it after me, then? And the spirit yesterday too?"

The woman's grin widened. "So self-flattering, these

lycan." She shook her head. "No, she found you on her own and brought you to me."

"And you're not curious why?"

"Perhaps I am."

"Can you ask her?" His head was foggy, but from everything he'd heard about the fae, they could speak to woodland creatures as easily as he was speaking to her now.

"I will, in time."

The trees at the edge of his vision dimmed once more as Hugh's head spun. He crunched the leaves beneath his palms as he balled his hands into a fist to refocus, growling under his breath.

"You've received quite a blow to the head, hmm?" She knelt down and peered at his wound.

"You should know the answer to that," he groaned.

The woman laid her staff on the ground and placed her hands on either side of his face. Her touch was cool, and immediately, the pounding of his bloodstream slowed. The urge to transform into his wolf form drifted slowly away through the woods. *"Elenai,"* she said in a low voice. The soft kiss of an invisible spirit graced his brow, and the wound began to heal.

"Thank you, lady." He blinked to clear his vision and catch a closer look at her. The gold of her complexion was a covering of some sort. Ivory skin with a silver glow peeked out from underneath the gilded flecks.

"What is it that you and your people are doing here, Hugh of the lycan?"

He chuckled. "If only I could give you a clear answer, mistress." He turned his gaze to the soft blue of the sky. "Fenrir instructed me to lead, and here we are. He said the path would be difficult, but if we could find a way to survive, eventually we would be able to make a home here and shape a new world."

The fae smiled. "Your god is vague, though he makes hefty promises."

The center of her lips were a dark rose pink beneath the gold covering. The shimmering powder was denser along her fingers, which looked solid gold, than it was over the delicate curves of her face. Long stretches of ivory skin hid beneath the leaves and vines of her garments.

"Do your gods speak plainly to you, and ours alone speaks in riddles?"

"I suppose that depends upon the one to whom we speak." She looked away. The verdant light of the forest darted across her features as she studied the woods. "For myself, I prefer to find answers elsewhere." She stood and placed her palm against the oak tree. "In the Brightlands, the gods spoke differently. I could feel them in the earth and air." A landscape of invisible memories spread across her features, tugging her away from the forest around them.

How plain must this woodland that he and his people found so mesmerizing, so abundant, seem to her? "That sounds magical," he said finally.

"Most things are."

Hugh grinned. His senses had calmed enough for him to trust his feet once more. He pushed himself up from the ground and knocked the dirt off of his jacket and breeches. "Might I ask your name again, forest mistress?"

"Lilia." She smiled.

Gods. "Daughter of the queen of the Enid?"

"Yes." Her eyes flashed, laughing at him, and once again, she turned to disappear into the forest.

"Wait!" Hugh yelled after her. "Why do you keep showing yourself to me?"

She paused, her profile in sharp contrast to the trees behind. "That we will have to see, Hugh of the lycan." The white doe thundered out of the woods and stopped before her. She placed her bare foot in a vine strung around its side and swung herself onto its back before the two of them tore away into the depths of the forest.

CHAPTER 7

TEODRIC

Teodric peered around the towering bookshelves, searching for Iellieth among the tomes. Scrawling quills and the slow turn of heavy pages mingled with the ink, candle wax, and dust of the Librarium. At small tables interspersed throughout the space, scholars hunched over their work. He found her in the brightest corner of the library, near one of the roaring fireplaces. Katarina leaned back and forth between an ancient book and a small stack of parchment spread across her lap. Iellieth stared out the window at the glow of the Arboretum's leaves. Teodric grinned. They were each lost in the worlds they conjured—Katarina's of words, Iellieth's of her drifting imagination.

He hid behind a bookshelf for a moment, watching them. From this angle, it was difficult to tell if Iellieth's lower lip was downturned in worry or if it was a trick of the light. She seemed tired. How greatly was the night before—or the worries of the nights still to come— weighing on her?

He cleared his throat as he approached to avoid startling them from their stories. "Pardon me, great Celestial translators, might I interrupt your work to suggest a turn around the grounds?" Iellieth's eyes widened, and Katarina's creased in a smile.

The scholar pursed her lips and laid her stack of parchment on top of the open tome. "I thank you for your kind offer, but I am afraid that I cannot join you." Katarina nodded to Iellieth. "We're set for the day, and I'll have new texts for you tomorrow. Why don't you leave those pages with me for now, and I'll see you then?"

Iellieth's hands lingered over the small sheaf of ever-green-inked pages. "Yes, Katarina, thank you." She picked up her box of inks and quills and moved toward a stack of books on the table.

"Can I help you with any of that?" Teodric scooped up two of the larger books and reached for the box. Iellieth balanced her elbow against her hip while he slowly pried the handle from her fingers.

While she had been out that morning, Teodric had paid a visit to the Amastacia wing to ask the duchess if Iellieth would be free that afternoon to help him with the song he was writing for the next gala.

He had been prepared to be rebuffed, but Duchess Amastacia was surprisingly pleased by the idea. "Try and get her to spend some time outside. She'll be cheered by the fresh air."

"As you wish, Your Grace." Teodric bowed and made his way to the library to find her.

The song that had started in the greenhouse and come into full bloom in the Arboretum the night before continued to traipse through his mind as he led Iellieth back to her family wing. He skipped ahead, sliding in front of her. "What do you say to spending the afternoon in the Arboretum?"

Her eyebrows rose in her excitement, and she rushed past him to return her tools to her room.

His father's warning had given him more time to reflect on the duke's plans than she, but even so, only a few alternatives had presented themselves. Today, in her favorite place on the castle grounds, he would try to convince her that the most promising path forward would be leaving Io Keep entirely—and he didn't want her to go alone.

IELLIETH

Iellieth smiled up at her favorite oak tree, the willow fronds waving in the breeze, as she and Teodric settled beneath the canopy of scarlet leaves. The events of the evening before sat heavily between them, a third guest shaded by the boughs. Teodric picked at the fringe of a blanket. The oak tree waited quietly overhead.

"Should I have foreseen his plan?" She spoke softly. This question seemed the easiest to answer from the cawing flock that flapped around her mind.

Slowly, Teodric met her gaze. "No, Iellieth." He sighed. "If you were more like him, then perhaps his plot would have been more obvious. But you don't approach the world with a scheme to advance your own desires at the expense of everyone else."

Her favorite heroines often forged plans that sought to shape their world, though their aims were usually to seek justice or explore the world's beauty. Should she be more like them? The tree's whispers overhead soothed her inner scolding. "Maybe I should form a plot of my own." She scrunched her lips to the side. Her pulse quickened. "One to counter his. That would be unexpected, and exciting . . ." But what would such a plan entail? Faeries, princesses, and explorers swirled before her. What would they do in her present circumstances? "He's going to keep bringing suitors here, isn't he?"

Teodric's jaw twinged, and he nodded.

"We already know better than to expect him to change his mind." She fiddled with her father's amulet, tracing its gold tines that surrounded a bright, beveled ruby gemstone. What would he have wanted for a daughter he had never met, whom he didn't know existed? Iellieth gasped. *That was it. What better time to find out?* "I'm going to the Realms."

"What?" Teodric pushed himself off his elbow and leaned toward her.

Shortly after they met, Iellieth had told him of her hopes of one day finding her father, the elven diplomat who had won her mother's heart, for a short while, seventeen years ago. He only needed to see that it would be better, in the long run, for her to go now and not wait. "In *Lady of Canis*, Daphne leaves her uncle's house behind when he tries to force her into marriage. I would be doing the same thing, except I have somewhere to go. She didn't."

He frowned. "Alright, so in this case—"

"I would be like Daphne, but on a quest to find my father instead of sheltering with a pack of wolves. I just need to find a way to board a ship that's crossing the ocean." Iellieth bit her lip. Would the duke be expecting her to try to run away? And how could she convince a captain to allow her on board? Very few would want to cross someone as powerful as her stepfather.

"And once you booked passage, you would sail to the Realms?"

Nerves fluttered in her stomach. "Yes." She frowned. "Do you know how I would go about finding a ship that would take me? And what would it cost?"

Her breath caught as Teodric suddenly seized her hand. "I don't know." His eyes softened beneath his knitted brow. "But I promise you that I will help you find out."

CHAPTER 8

TEODRIC

Over the next few weeks, Teodric helped Iellieth plan her escape from Io Keep. He had been relieved that she so quickly settled upon leaving the castle entirely, but they were still struggling to find a way for her to cross the ocean. His stomach turned each time he rehearsed the litany of threats that a young, inexperienced noblewoman might encounter on her travels. Added to this, the passage to the Realms was notoriously dangerous. Few beyond bands of pirates were brave enough to sail the unchartered waters, a vast sea teeming with ancient monsters of the deep, plagued by vicious storms. Linolynn's traders and warships clung to the coastline of Caldara. His father had said that one in two ships that set sail for the other side of the world never returned. For the time being, they decided, she would find a destination that she could reach over land and then attempt her passage by sea.

Duke Amastacia had made moves of his own in the meantime, but they'd managed to dodge both of the suitors he put in Iellieth's path. For the first, a spot of luck revealed that the man was deathly afraid of spiders. One carefully arranged pillow-guest on behalf of him and Scad had sent the suitor packing.

The second was even easier. Katarina organized a special luncheon in the nobleman's honor and invited one of the visiting scholars from Hadvar to join them. By the end of the meal, the two were so besotted with each other that the nobleman cancelled the remainder of his trip to accompany the scholar on his return journey to the north.

Scad's extensive knowledge of the servants' passages helped as well. They explored several promising routes through the castle, and the three of them slowly gathered the supplies Iellieth would need on her journey.

She bounded into his room one mid-autumn afternoon, the scent of cinnamon from the kitchens and the musk of dried leaves from the Arboretum in her hair. "Katarina found a new map to help us plan."

Teodric waved her over, clearing away from his desk the sheet music he'd been transposing. He unfurled the map, revealing a detailed view of the central range of the Frostmaw Mountains and the roads that wound between them. They'd discussed her heading directly east or slightly north, but the mountains would offer more protection and obscured trails. His finger traced a winding route that led to Vestige Lake. "We could take this passage—" Teodric sucked in his breath, and Iellieth stilled beside him. They hadn't discussed him accompanying her, but in all the routes he'd suggested, he had imagined being by her side.

"We?" Iellieth stared back at him, the word balanced on the edge of her lips.

He didn't want to take it back now that he had finally said it. "Yes." His exhale was shallow. *Let me come with you.* He leaned closer. The gold sparks in her eyes shone back at him. Her hip rested against the desk near his hand, and her eyes danced across his face.

Iellieth turned back to the map. "We could certainly go that way. Would you want us to travel through Penshaw or Red's Cross before we continue over the mountains?"

He grinned. *We.* "Let's think about it and see. Some of it may depend on how soon we leave."

⚜

WHEN THEY WEREN'T TOGETHER SCHEMING, TEODRIC worked on the song he had heard that night in the gardens. Into it he poured the hope he couldn't risk speaking aloud.

The duchess continued to speak of potential matches, and Iellieth's time grew more filled with etiquette and the study of foreign courts and trade. Her mother crowded the court's spring schedule with visiting lords and dignitaries. Though most of the threats loomed several months away, a heaviness settled onto her shoulders, dampening her inner light. She was frightened, and she had every right to be. "We'll leave in a few weeks," Teodric declared, "and we'll reach the foothills before the first deep snows." His family had a few connections scattered across the base of the Frostmaws. He just needed enough time to send word to them so he and Iellieth would have places to shelter along the way.

Iellieth agreed. A few more weeks, and she would be safe from the duke's plans.

But ten days later, as a storm howled across the castle grounds, news rattled the windows of Io Keep and made its way to the Adhemar wing.

His father burst into his room, brow furrowed. Teodric

sank onto the edge of his bed. Duke Amastacia was entertaining a troupe of Hadvarian noblemen, including a young man from one of the city-state's wealthiest and most powerful families. Lord Anderson Duchevsky had accepted the invitation to the castle, and Iellieth would be accompanying him to a ball in his honor the next evening. Frederick paused.

Teodric could scarcely gather the strength to look his father in the eye. "Tell me," he croaked, hand shoved back through his hair.

"By all accounts, the duke intends for Lady Iellieth to be betrothed the following morning and married shortly thereafter." His father turned his gaze to the floor. "I'm sorry, son."

Teodric nodded, the inside of his bottom lip wedged firmly between his teeth. He cleared his throat, carving out just enough room for words to pass. "You and Mother know that I love you."

His father nodded. "We do." Frederick crossed the room, wrapped his arms around his son's shoulders, and bent to whisper in his ear. "And we're incredibly proud of you." He kissed the top of Teodric's head and left the room.

Teodric glared out at the gusts that roiled the dark gray sea, the cries of the waves echoing those of his heart. They would have two days, at best, to put their plan into motion.

CHAPTER 9

IELLIETH

A soft knock brought Iellieth to her door. "Mamaun, what is it?" Worry creased her mother's brow, and the small smile she had managed kept twisting toward a grimace.

"You and I will spend the day together," Mamaun said softly.

Iellieth's heart fluttered. Something was wrong. "But I have plans with Katarina today. We're working on—"

"Calderon has arranged a special gala this evening for Lord Anderson Duchevsky of Hadvar."

Her blood ran cold and began to pound against her ears, drowning out her mother's voice.

"You will accompany him to the event." Iellieth opened her mouth to protest, but her mother interrupted her. "And you will have no guests between now and then."

Mamaun swept into her room and bolted the latch across the servants' door. She drew herself up to full height. "Bridget will be nearby to attend to you." In a sweep of long skirts, she rustled out the door.

After a shaky breath, Iellieth ran down the hall after

her mother and caught the duchess's arm. "Mamaun, I don't want to do this again." Tears stung her eyes. They weren't ready, not yet. "Please."

Was it anger or sadness that pulled at her mother's lips? Before she could decipher the expression, Mamaun yanked her arm away, and Iellieth stumbled, off balance. "This is what you've been preparing for." The duchess spun away, heels clicking sharply against the polished wooden floorboards.

You have no idea what I've been preparing for, Iellieth thought.

Her mother's voice rose at the end of the hall, directing members of the family guard to station themselves outside her room. Iellieth clasped her father's amulet and ran back into her raided sanctuary. A heavy fog draped across the sea, blotting out the line of the horizon. She would be trapped if they didn't find some way to succeed.

Bridget arrived a short while later with a scarlet silk dress her mother had specifically commissioned from Henri for the occasion. The vibrant fabric gleamed across Iellieth's pale skin and brought out dark threads of garnet that wound through her red hair. The makeup was simpler this time, emphasizing her bright green eyes and letting the low neckline, tight bodice, and full skirt speak for themselves.

The day passed in a slow swirl of dread. However closely she watched, the sun never emerged from the swollen gray clouds. She and her mother descended into the ballroom. The duke glowered, posturing before a group of young, finely dressed noblemen, most of whom had dark hair and richly tanned complexions.

As she rose from her curtsy, Iellieth immediately identified Lord Duchevsky among the crowd. While the others looked at her shyly, or with the soft blush of attraction, he observed her every movement with a sharp hunger, scowling at his friends nearby as though someone else would swoop in and claim his prize.

The little food she'd managed to eat turned in her stomach.

Her stepfather smirked as he introduced them, his expression that of a taunting jester who might burst into peals of laughter at any moment. Lord Duchevsky bent to kiss her hand and then turned and nodded to the duke, his approval writ plain.

Iellieth balled her free hand into a fist to prevent its shaking. The silk of her dress was of no aid to the sudden clammy sweat of her palms. Flashes of the last gala fizzled before her. Her heart slowed at the memory of sitting outside with her head on Teodric's shoulder. She wouldn't be able to escape this evening so easily. Her mother's eyes skittered away from her and rested nervously on the duke. Was she not fond of the match either but unwilling to say so? Iellieth stared at the duchess, silently begging her to reconsider. Mamaun turned away to speak with one of the other guests, and Lord Duchevsky led her out onto the floor.

After the first dance, he retired and handed her off to one of his party of Hadvarian noblemen. She couldn't slow her mind long enough to catch the man's name when he introduced himself. A second Iellieth—the one who dreamed of visiting Vestige Lake, of sailing to the Elven Realms to find her father, who had been forced again to miss her morning of translations with Katarina—watched from the wall in silent horror as the trapped Iellieth spun from one stranger to another across the shimmering ballroom.

Lord Duchevsky sat at the edge of the floor, elbows propped on his knees when he wasn't gulping deep draughts of wine, observing her, a calculating glint in his eyes. The duke glared at her as well, though with different aims. Iellieth-on-the-wall couldn't decide which was worse. Dancing-Iellieth knew it didn't matter.

A second unknown companion of Lord Duchevsky came and replaced the first. Even with her back turned, alternating parts of her body shivered away from the Hadvarian's gaze—her neck, her waist, her breast, her wrists. The nobleman didn't speak to his party, as far as she could tell. He expressed his wishes in rapid hand gestures or agitated, almost violent facial expressions.

Iellieth squinted at Duchevsky's companions. Had they ever hosted a group of dignitaries who traveled without any women? Duchevsky and his followers didn't even travel with a family elder or steward. Did his judgments depend solely on himself, his companions, and her stepfather?

Like his predecessor, this partner was quiet. The music slowed to a waltz, and Iellieth's thoughts calmed. Perhaps Teodric knew about this surprise suitor already and had been able to alter their plans. Or, if not, he could ready something for the following evening. The duke wouldn't risk the perceived impropriety of an immediate engagement *and* wedding. Mamaun wouldn't let him . . . would she? Iellieth couldn't bring herself to look at either of them.

The waltz ended, and the doors at the far end of the ballroom swung open. Teodric entered with Lord and Lady

Adhemar, but without one of his mother's carefully selected matches on his arm. Iellieth shifted around her new, inordinately tall Hadvarian, trying to catch Teodric's eye. Her heart faltered, unable to wait and choose a moment when Lord Duchevsky wasn't looking, if such a chance existed.

Teodric's shoulders grew rigid when he spotted her. So he had an idea of the duke's plans. Slowly, he made his way across the room, speaking with other nobles, nodding politely to their conversations, his eyes never wavering as he carved a meandering path to her side.

TEODRIC

The duke's gaze burrowed a pit through Teodric's gut from the moment he walked through the ballroom doors. Iellieth twirled at the far end of the brightly lit hall, radiant in a rich ruby gown the identical shade as the gem in her treasured amulet. His sight narrowed, shoving its way across the floor to read her expression. The lanky fellow she danced with couldn't be her soon-to-be-betrothed. Her upper lip turned, a slight pout of worry, but not as pronounced as it would have been were this her suitor.

A blade sank into his stomach when he found Lord Duchevsky over Duke Amastacia's shoulder. The nobleman eyed Iellieth with aggressive possession, eyes caressing the curves of her shape. Teodric moved closer, sliding past a knot of nobles. Duchevsky snapped his fingers at one of the servants, his hand curling into a fist as he scolded the young woman. Her face pale in fright, she returned a few moments later, the tray shaking as she brought out some of the castle's finest wine. Iellieth's suitor, his eyes locked on his prey, didn't even acknowledge the woman's return. One of his well-dressed minions snatched the tray from her hands, poured his liege a glass of wine, and placed the thin stem between Duchevsky's burly fingers.

Teodric peered around the ballroom for the golden glow of Duchess Amastacia's hair in the torchlight. Surely she wouldn't allow her daughter to be sent away, married off to such a brute. Cold sweat beaded across Teodric's back. Had Iellieth ever mentioned her mother standing up to the duke? He found his own mother in the crowd, but her closest friend wasn't by her side.

Finally he spied her by the row of glass doors he had helped Iellieth through at the last ball. Duchess Amastacia stood unmoving, her back to the room, staring at the raging winds that swept through the trees outside. Her reflection in the glass was strained. She wore her long hair in a tight bun at the base of her neck, and her hand clawed into the marble doorframe to steady her. But would she do nothing else?

As no other alternatives emerged before him, Teodric readied himself to request Iellieth's next dance and see if she could leave that night. He and Scad had spent the day preparing and, if all had gone according to plan, Scad was in Iellieth's room now, checking the contents of her hidden bag against Teodric's list and adding her dark green cloak to the items she'd already packed. Scad would also ensure she had traveling clothes of some sort—there was no way for her to blend in even in the Air Ward in her close-fitting red dress.

His heart burned as he glared at Duchevsky again. The

man's open regard for Iellieth was understandable, but he longed to knock the undisguised ardor directly from the Hadvarian's face. Iellieth deserved better—deserved someone whom, his heart whispered, she just might grow to love in return.

CHAPTER 10

TEODRIC

As the final notes of the concerto rang out, Teodric slid across the ballroom floor, appearing next to Iellieth and the Hadvarian gentleman she'd been dancing with. "Might I cut in?"

The man looked surprised but assented, having no cause to refuse without risking rudeness. Iellieth's partner returned to the group of visiting noblemen. Duchevsky's glare joined her stepfather's.

Teodric took Iellieth's chilled hand and wrapped his arm firmly around her waist.

She smiled up at him, her eyes shining. "Thank you."

Every muscle in his body longed to whisk her out of the ballroom and away into the stormy night. The longer they stayed, the more the danger grew—he could feel it in his pulse beating against his chest. "You look beautiful tonight, Iellieth." Green irises gleamed back at him. The music swept them up into its embrace, and he guided her around the ballroom, spinning in and out of the others waltzing across the floor. "Do you want to run away tonight . . . with me?" The song's undulating crescendos afforded them the perfect opportunity to talk without fear of being overheard.

Iellieth was flushed from the dance, her chest rising and falling quickly. "I couldn't ready anything today." Her brow creased. "Mamaun constantly had someone nearby."

"Scad is working on that right now," he whispered. "And don't worry, he's being very careful. I made sure it would be safe for him to get through." He spun her out, pulse pounding for her answer until she returned.

"I would love to leave with you tonight, Teodric." Sparkles of crystal flickered across her face.

He pulled her closer, his stomach dropping at the catch in her breath. "The song you've heard me working on . . ." If ever there were a time, it was now. "I wrote it for you." A pulse beat at the base of her neck, but he couldn't look at her expression, not yet. "I'll find you for your song"— her cheeks lifted in a smile—"and then we'll split up and meet in the hall like we planned."

His hand followed the fluid movement of her waist as she sighed. "I'm so . . . relieved." Iellieth squeezed his hand, her voice even softer. "I've been frightened all day. Mamaun, the duke, they both seem more serious this time. And—" She shivered. They were too close to her suitor again. He spun her away.

"After tonight, we'll put all of this behind us, and you won't have to worry about the duke anymore. You'll be safe, and we'll go far away." His grip tightened around her, as though that alone were enough to ward off anything that might go wrong. "I promise."

MASTER BERGMAN, THE COURT CONDUCTOR, APPEARED at Teodric's elbow at the apex of the evening. "Sir Adhemar"—he bowed—"we shall play your song at the close of the next set if that is still agreeable to you?"

"Yes, sir." Teodric bowed in return. "And you'll include the dedication to my parents, as we discussed?"

"Of course." A deep nod, and the two parted.

The music master had been unhappy at his request that the orchestra play his original composition without him, but Teodric had cautiously explained that it was his parents' expectation for him to dance as much as he was able during the surprise gala. Reluctantly, Master Bergman consented.

The gentle melodies of the first several songs in the set drifted by with him unable to find a handhold to pull himself into their lulling embrace. One after another of Duchevsky's men danced with Iellieth, the Hadvarian always looking on with narrow-eyed interest. Teodric downed a glass of sparkling champagne to calm his nerves and took his mother for a turn about the floor.

Lights winked off the ringlets of her dark hair. "Are you happy here, Mother?" She had dreamt of moving to Io Keep for so long—how could she ever understand someone wanting to leave it? His father guessed the truth, but he doubted she had any notion of his plans. Father would explain it to her, eventually. Teodric's throat tightened. When would he next see her?

His mother's eyes drifted from the swirling crowd to his face. She placed a gloved hand against the line of his jaw. "I am, sweetheart. I know that you and your father miss Forestvale, but we belong here." She smiled. "You belong here. Your father and I, we only want what's best for you."

Their song came to a close, and Teodric's heart swelled. "I know that, Mother." He kissed the back of her hand. "I know how hard you've both worked, what you sacrificed, to make our life here a reality."

She squeezed his hand, beaming at him in reply. Frederick approached and patted him on the back before sweeping into a deep bow. "Might I have this dance, my dear?" Aurelia giggled as she curtsied, and his father carried her off into the first chords of the waltz.

Master Bergman cleared his throat at the song's close, tapping his baton for the court's attention. "Ladies and gentlemen, Your Graces, it is my great pleasure to present a new song to you tonight, written by our very own Sir Teodric Adhemar, and dedicated to his commendable parents, Lady and Lord Adhemar." Polite applause rippled across the ballroom, and his mother's eyes misted over with tears. His father's shoulders drew back—he was glowing with pride. Teodric smiled at both of them, his own vision blurred. Would they ever forgive him? Two people who had fallen in love and been allowed to be together—could they possibly understand?

A hand wrapped around his elbow, and his gaze swept up the silky red lines of Iellieth's gown to her face. She watched him expectantly, her lips curved in a small grin, but behind it was the same unease that he felt at the new world of possibilities opening before them. "Do you still want to dance with me?" Her head tilted as she waited for his answer, amused excitement twinkling across her expression.

"More than anything." Teodric took her in his arms, and the song he'd written for her began. Here on the cusp of their escape, in a moment he'd rehearsed countless times in his mind, he allowed the open regard he felt for

Iellieth to show. It radiated from every inch of his person, concentrated on the delicate contours of her face. There had been so many tiny acts of bravery—from first speaking to her when he'd recently arrived to live in Io Keep to their excursions through secret passages or forged trails in the Arboretum, to every moment when he'd imagined precisely this—the two of them, together, his heart bared for her to see.

He had rewritten the lyrics over and over again, struggling to land upon the precise words to tell her how he felt, how to go about saying something that had been said so often before but existed anew for every soul that fell in love.

The slow melody allowed him to hold her close. He lowered his head and softly sang into her ear, his voice a quiet echo of the tenors and bassists. The early verses recounted the story of a young man who arrived in a beautiful forest, initially believing himself to be alone. But as he walked deeper in, he found a dryad who already called the forest her home.

Iellieth tightened her hold on his hand, her heels rising and falling with the cascading notes of the song.

Immediately smitten, the man searched far and wide through the forest, seeking a gift that would express all he longed to say to the dryad, something that would prove him worthy, that would show her his devotion. He wandered into a sunlit glade where a lone, dark red flower bloomed in the middle of a circle of trees. The man plucked the flower, believing it would be the perfect gift for the dryad, who immediately emerged, green eyes blazing at the affront to her forest.

Iellieth's breath was warm against his neck. She loved stories, especially tales of the fae. Casting her as a beautiful dryad, like the legend of Hugh and Lilia she'd read snippets of from Katarina's translations, was the best way he knew to tell her, in words she would understand and believe, how he felt.

The man in the ballad fell to his knees, begging her forgiveness, and sang of his love, offering his heart to the dryad in place of the flora he'd taken from the glade.

> *The breath of spring, chill of autumn*
> *Brought to me by good Fortune*

When he'd practiced the melody the sea gave him after her first suitor, testing the words, his voice would crack before the final chorus as he tried to transition into the dryad's portion of the melody. After the first few days, he began to understand that he couldn't include the dryad's answer as part of the song—it would be up to Iellieth to answer for her.

The vision of finally being able to tell her how he felt still overwhelmed most of his evening practices as he plucked away at his lute. But tonight, intensified by their impending departure and the dizzying rush of holding her close, the song emerged perfectly, each word finding its home with her, carrying the melody of his love.

> *I have dreamt of this moment for years*
> *Of you, loved in my arms, all these years*

The man in the ballad spoke of falling in love with the dryad, over and over again, as he walked through the forest and learned its ways. Finding her, he explained, a creature of legend, had been nearly impossible in the first place, and he knew he would never find someone like her again.

However much he wished to, Teodric couldn't draw back and meet Iellieth's eyes during the song. The verses and chorus needed to work together to cast the spell of revealing his heart. Since he had first heard of the duke's plans for her future, and even before, when his father had cautioned him against forming an attachment, this had been brewing inside him, and he couldn't let even her reaction unravel what had been so carefully wrought.

Teodric had reminded himself, as the song grew and matured within him, that even if Iellieth were absolutely sure of her feelings one way or another, she would want time to think it over, to carefully examine each facet before allowing the gem out into the world beyond her internal light.

> *Breathe deeply in this moment*
> *that holds us together*
> *Forevermore, I'm yours*
> *to keep, to hold, ever yours*

The song faded, and Teodric willed the world around them to be still, if only for a moment. The ballroom held its breath. He searched the beat of her pulse, the rhythm of her breath to speak the words he longed to hear. But first, he had a final message to relay. He leaned closer, the edge of his lips grazing her ear. "I love you, Iellieth. I'll see you in two hours."

He stepped back, clutching her hand, and bowed. She stood rapt, a question poised behind her eyes. Teodric smiled and left the ballroom, striding back to the Adhemar wing.

CHAPTER 11

IELLIETH

The attendees applauded as Teodric left the ballroom, the intricate melody and inventive verse structure sure to make his song for her a favorite among the Linolynnian court. Iellieth stood dazed, rooted to the ballroom floor, rehearsing each moment in her mind. Another of Lord Duchevsky's companions appeared before her to take her hand for the new set.

Iellieth's head had already been spinning after Teodric told her he'd written a song for her that they would dance to, but that he loved her—she took a step back as though trying to catch the full vision of the two of them in a mirror. She had guessed at his feelings and long suppressed any of her own at Mamaun's strict warning, but what did it mean now that it was said and they were planning to run away together? Was this a more complicated freedom, or a stronger wave of what she had already desired?

Her body danced without her conscious thought for the rest of the evening, and her mind oscillated between Teodric singing to her and selecting the perfect moment to leave the ball. Various nobles and attendants had begun to depart for the evening, a trend that would help her case. She would only need to give a convincing performance of her regard for Lord Duchevsky and avoid any displays of relief that the duke could see.

She held up a hand to the next of his men who approached her and turned to speak with her suitor. "My Lord, you must excuse me." Bile rose in her throat as he stared back at her. A short while longer, and she would be free. "I am most tired from this evening's festivities and must retire." She bit down on her lip, the words from her etiquette lessons rising unbidden. Perhaps, just this once, they would help. "I hope you enjoyed yourself, and I look forward to seeing you on the morrow." Her longing to depart kept the bite from her voice.

Lord Duchevsky looked from her to where her stepfather stood nearby. "You dance beautifully, Lady Amastacia. We shall speak in the morning." Iellieth clamped her teeth shut and nodded. She couldn't react to the nobleman's roving gaze across her body. Her stepfather walked to the edge of the ring of Duchevsky's entourage. "You and I"— Duchevsky glanced at the duke—"we will work out the particulars then."

Her stepfather bowed. "As you wish, Lord Duchevsky." What a repulsive pair they made, scheming and fawning with no regard for herself or her feelings on the matter. They might as well have been discussing terms over land or horses. To them, they were.

Her stomach plummeted. Iellieth stepped away. So long as the duke didn't follow her, or send one of his guards to do so, she could escape.

Mamaun was watching her from the back of the ballroom, lips slightly pursed. Her mother's sapphire eyes glimmered as she approached. Did she know? How much did the relief and excitement she felt show in her bearing and on her face? As they had planned, Iellieth had considered leaving a note for Mamaun, trying to explain why she had to flee. But she couldn't ask the questions she longed to have answered. *Why did you stop caring for me? Why did you turn me over to him? Was it something I did?* Such questions would either hurt Mamaun or enflame the duke's anger even further. She knew that her escape, more even than her very existence, would remind him of a time when Mamaun nearly broke free.

She curled her hands behind her back and curtsied to her mother. "Good night, Mamaun." Memories of her mother's smile at her, the brightness that once shimmered in her face when she watched her young half-elven daughter, sputtered to life in Iellieth's heart. With a quick breath, she rose and placed a kiss on her mother's cheek.

"Iellieth . . ." Mamaun started to speak but drew back. A cold shadow appeared over Iellieth's shoulder. The duke had followed her.

She squeezed her mother's hand. "Excuse me."

Would she ever see Mamaun again? Was a new path forward in their relationship a possibility on some distant horizon she couldn't yet see? There was no time to worry about that now. Iellieth kept her steps slow, walking calmly to her room. If anyone were following her, they would have no sense that something was amiss.

Not till they found her missing the next morning.

A THUMP SOUNDED AGAINST THE FLOOR OF HER ROOM AS she unlatched the door. "Who's—"

"Shh." Scad's head emerged from the other side of the bed. He rose as she locked the door behind her, having thrown himself onto the ground in his attempt to hide.

Iellieth rushed forward and embraced her friend. "I didn't realize I would get to see you. How did you—" The bolt to the servants' passage hung loose, partially broken from the door.

"I had a little bit of help." Scad shrugged, a small smile flitting across his lips. "Oh!" He jumped forward. "I almost forgot." He turned to her desk and handed her a bundle about the length of her forearm, wrapped in a silk scarf.

"What is it?"

"Be careful!" Scad pulled the scarf back, his eyes wide. "Teodric wanted you to have it just in case. But he said it's really sharp." He extended the object again and placed it flat on her palms.

Teodric's dagger gleamed in the moonlight beneath the floral scarf. Almost every day she'd seen him, he carried the blade somewhere on his person. "One must be always on the cusp of adventure," he had said with a wink. Intertwining vines, or tangled roots, curled across its length, their pattern accentuating the gleaming edge of the blade. Arching limbs stretched across the wooden hilt in the sprawling golden oak of the Adhemar crest, delicately inlaid with silver leaves.

Scad's head bent over as he studied the dagger. "You're not going to need to use that, are you, Ellie?"

She grinned and shook her head. "No, I don't think so, Scad. It's a symbol more than anything else."

"And"—he sniffled and bit down on his lips—"you promise that you'll help me find a way to meet you . . . in a year or two?"

Iellieth's chest swelled. Scad had many friends in the

castle, but their friendship was special, on both sides. "I promise, Scad."

He slipped out of the servants' door, and Iellieth began to pace, trying to calm her nerves for the night ahead. Muffled voices down the hall signaled Mamaun and the duke's return. She jumped over and blew out the candles closest to the door and fumbled at the clasps to her dress. Her leggings and warm tunic waited beside a bag in her bottom drawer. What was she supposed to say if someone saw her in the corridors with a pack? She had to tend to something in the Arboretum? Why would they believe that? Iellieth laced her boots. Once they were out of the castle, she could put on her traveling cloak.

Teodric's voice drifted back, enveloping her in his embrace. What was she going to say when she saw him? He wouldn't expect her to answer right away. Sometimes, after seeing the kind, beautiful women his mother selected for him for each of the balls, she had thought . . . A warm glow flared to life in the center of her being, the opening of a fire flower. *He loved her. And they were leaving Io Keep, together.*

Iellieth stood and grabbed her bag. Her breath trembled at the base of her throat. She slipped out of her door and crept toward the servants' passage beside the duke's study, the last one they would think to check. Teodric would be waiting for her on the other side of the circuitous route Scad had mapped out.

The hallway was clear of any servants or family members. She cast one final glance over her shoulder and ducked into the narrow passageway.

CHAPTER 12

TEODRIC

Teodric's fingers twitched, strings of invisible notes darting through the air. They had agreed that he would wait for her around the corner from the portrait door, but the hallways were especially dim this evening, the castle itself lending its aid to their cause. She shouldn't have to venture down the dark hallway alone. He leaned against the wall's stony shadows, his heart pounding in his ears.

With a low creak, the portrait inched open into the hallway, and Iellieth's shoes gently tapped against the stone floor. Teodric raised his finger to his lips and slowly stepped toward her, sliding into the dim torchlight of the passageway.

His stomach lurched at the look in her eyes. A light gleamed behind her smile that spoke of something beyond her relief that they were leaving the castle. His pulse beat faster as she took his hand in hers. Teodric pulled her into his chest, the sweet musk of peonies and roses drifting off her hair. "Did you make it here alright?" A nod beneath his chin. "Did anyone follow you?" The silk of her hair swished back and forth across his hand. He sighed. "Are you ready?"

"Yes," she whispered. Her infectious grin reflected across his face. Tonight would be the last that she was courted against her will, the end of the duke asserting his power over her. He raised her hand to his lips and planted a kiss across the back of it, a promise of things to come. They crept along the side of the passage hand-in-hand and tiptoed around the corner where he had emerged a half hour before. Only three corridors stood between them and the exterior walls of Io Keep.

His heartbeat pounded in his ears. Soon, they would be free.

A shadow shifted in the periphery. Iellieth gasped, and her hand slipped from his. Teodric spun, reaching back for her. She flailed against a hulking shape, a gloved hand clamped around her mouth. "Iellieth!" Teodric dove back toward her, and a second figure emerged from the darkness. The man's meaty fist collided with his stomach, another with his head. The shapes in the shadows muffled Iellieth's screams.

A sudden beam of moonlight crossed the hall. He cried out, a flash of white as a boot struck the side of his knee. Bright green eyes shone back at him, creased along the edges, blazing with pain and terror. The crack of broken ribs. Teodric coughed against the blood that clogged his throat.

Curled strands of dark red hair framed the side of her face. A brutal force splintered across the back of his head. Darkness.

IELLIETH

Iellieth stopped struggling once she saw Teodric fall, afraid that further resistance on her part would lead to additional violence against his prone form. Sobs shook her body, her cries still muted by the first brute who had seized her, and the eight guards marched down the castle corridors back to the Amastacia wing, carrying her and leaving Teodric where he lay.

The steward, Sir Merud, opened the door and gestured for them to hurry inside. The private soldiers transported Iellieth down the hall to her room and placed her on her bed. Her stepfather loomed in the doorway, and they stood at attention. His slender frame slunk into the room, shaking in rage as he glared down at her.

The duke's eyes flashed to the one who had clamped his palm over her face. The bruises from his hand were already beginning to swell. "It's done, Your Grace," the guard said.

Her stepfather nodded in reply. "You may leave us." His nasal voice hissed more than usual, threat emanating from his bearing. The guard he had spoken to glanced at Iellieth and began to question the order, but a twitch in her stepfather's lip silenced the impulse, and the guards filed out.

Iellieth gripped the blankets to stop her hands from shaking. Anger, not fear, would serve her now. How had he known?

The duke glowered from across the room, his eyes glittering in the darkness. If he drew too close to her, she would run out into the hall. She'd never known him to raise his own hand in violence, but if ever there were a first time, this might be it. "I am relieved you've returned safely." His cold voice pierced the room. Iellieth's jaw clamped tighter.

He tucked his arms behind his back and stepped nearer, his shadow stretched by the lanterns in the hallway. "The boy will live—my guards are careful, despite what powers the castle grants me to protect those in my charge from kidnappings." A howl of wind swept past outside. Iellieth squeezed her grip tighter. What she wouldn't give for the ability to lash out at her stepfather, to be rid of him and his schemes forever.

"But hear me plainly." The windowpanes quaked against the wind. The duke glanced nervously outside and then returned his beady sights to her. "Should you ever try something like that again, anyone accompanying you, whoever they are, will not be so lucky. Do you understand?"

Iellieth stared at the wall, the image of Teodric lying still and bloody in the hall burned into her eyes. She never would be able to escape. The chance wasn't worth Teodric's life, or Scad's. The wind outside her windows calmed, its arms draped around her shoulders. *Keep waiting and watching*, the wind whispered. Silence in answer to her stepfather's threats was the one rebellion left to her in this moment. *You will find another way*. Iellieth narrowed her eyes. She would simply act alone in the future.

The dagger Teodric had given her pressed its reassurance against her ankle, and her amulet glowed warm across her chest. She wouldn't be alone after all.

Her stepfather's jaw worked side to side as he stared back at her. He took a step forward. The wind picked up again as Iellieth turned the narrow beam of her eyes to his. "I'll take that as a yes." His wide, thin lips twisted. "Know this. I will take any contact between the two of you, from this point forward, as a threat to our family's assets and dispose of him accordingly. The same as I did to your bastard father." Iellieth gasped. No one had ever said that her father—

The duke chuckled and rolled his shoulders back. "And just as before, the . . . temptation will not exist for much longer. I am sending the Adhemars away." He brushed his hands together and stepped toward the door. "Remember what I've said. You really don't want more blood on your hands, do you?" He pulled a shiny gold key from his waist-coat pocket and wiggled it so that it captured the light. A last peal of laughter, and the door clicked shut behind him, the outer lock thudding into place.

CHAPTER 13

TEODRIC

A soft voice pulled Teodric out of the haze. Mauve lips formed foggy, incoherent words beneath orbs of dark brown. "Katarina?" A warm hand squeezed his shoulder.

"Yes. Lie still."

Teodric squinted. Walls of mist coated the world around him, the edges of the room little more than blurs of muted color. A flash of memory—the guards pulling Iellieth away from him. He groaned as he tried to sit up. "Where is she?"

Katarina pressed against his chest, forcing him to lie back on the bed. "Iellieth is alright, but she's locked in her room." Her whisper floated on a breeze as the fog began to lift. "You won't be able to see her."

"I have to." His voice was dry, cracked. She couldn't stay here. They had to leave. He cried out at the spasm of pain that bolted up his leg as he tried to move. His knee. They'd broken it in his fight to escape.

"Hold still." Katarina cupped both her hands around

his knee. She murmured words he did not understand, waves crashing upon rocks.

Teodric shut his eyes. The song he'd written for Iellieth pressed her anxious hands against the walls of his heart. *Did we not succeed?* He couldn't tell her, not yet.

Katarina's speech returned to Caldaran. "I can heal this, but it will take time."

Only the most powerful priests had access to healing magics. "You can—"

"*Shh.*" The tide of Katarina's voice pulled him beneath the surface. "There are more magics in this world than you yet know. Let me sing you a story, and the sea will take care of you." The words rose on an alto wave, conjuring the salty spray of a rising tide, lulling Teodric back toward the world of dreams. "There was once a young mermaid who lived in the city of Nepta, deep beneath the Infinite Ocean . . ."

⚜

THE MERMAID'S TALE

More than anything, the mermaid loved to sing. This was not necessarily unique to the mermaid, you see, but there was something distinctive about her songs. Unlike the sirens among her people, or the enchanting naiada, this mermaid sang not of the ocean depths but of the stars above.

Her parents were scholars of the celestial spheres. Her father was an explorer, her mother a mermaid. One night, a terrible storm threw the mermaid's father from his craft. He writhed against the power of the sea, but the goddess

Kleodna refused to release the man from her watery grasp. Fate tied him to her depths, and she tugged him below.

The mermaid's mother was swimming past, returning to Nepta from a long, arduous scouting mission through the southern seas. The young man's body drifted on a strong current. "I've brought you something," the goddess of the sea said to the young woman. The mermaid's mother was puzzled, but she held out her arms to receive the gift from Kleodna. She kissed the young man, granting him life, and a second chance to breathe, this time from the ocean's shimmering core.

The pair returned to the city, and the young man told the mermaid about the wonders of the world of the stars above. "There is a realm," he said, "where goddesses, gods, and ancient fae all roam. And I will take you there one day."

They had two children as they hatched these plans, in the days when the sea began to grow cold, and dark beings returned to lurk in the southern tides.

Few were as brave as the mermaid's mother had been, and they did not wish to patrol the far seas. "I must lead one final journey, my loves," the mother said.

The father's brow furrowed, but he did not tell her to stay. "The stars will be there when you return."

"And we'll walk them together, you and I." She smiled at her love and opened her arms to her mer-children. "Be brave, Aravar"—she kissed his head—"and continue to sing, my sweet Katarina." The mermaid kissed her mother's cheek.

They never saw her again.

Two sets of seasons passed, and the seas grew ever colder. The Neptan court summoned the father to their chambers. The mermaid and her brother helped him swim to reach the meeting in time. "She is not coming back," the mer-king said, "and the threats along our borders grow."

The mermaid began to cry. Her father held her head to his chest. She whispered up to him, "But what about the stars?" Her mother had loved them best, and she had taught young Katarina all their songs.

A sea witch was visiting the court at this time. She had the tall ears and large eyes of the ancient fae. "If I might intervene"—the witch pushed herself forward, clinging to the edge of her chair—"I will take the family above to live with me. Though they have lost much, they have still a great role to play."

She guided them to the world above the sea.

The mermaid learned to walk on the land. She began to travel, as both her parents had. She helped the witch with her potions, and she studied the stars overhead.

But she did not continue to sing.

Two years after they left the sea, the mermaid's father died, joining his wife in the starry realm of Astralei. The witch carried on the teachings of the children's parents, telling them about the wars that had raged to form Azuria, wars that would rise again one day. "It is in your path to help," the witch said. "Be ever watchful and brave."

Her sixteenth year, the mermaid held on to the witch and guided her out through the first waves of the sea. Smiling members of the mer-court waited there to receive them. They held out their hands to the witch, a promise to keep before she settled into her grave.

"Will I ever see you again?" the mermaid asked, tears stinging her eyes.

"You will, child." The witch cupped the girl's face.

"With your father and mother, on the starry plane of Astralei."

The mermaid helped the witch into the arms of the court, more tears gathering at the glitter of their scales. They sang to her, calling her back, but the siren in her heart had been dashed upon the rocks long ago.

She turned away with a vow that she would never look upon sea or stars again. The mermaid and her brother traveled underground, making their home with gnomes and dwarves in the Underland.

But however deep she traveled, in her dreams, the sea and stars still called. As she slept, the siren in her heart splashed her fins against crashing waves. She rested upon sun-warmed rocks, waiting for the twilight hours when the constellations would emerge to weave their stories for her once more.

Katarina was not alone in hearing these songs. In the Underland, small traveling bands also told the stories of wind and waves, of the workings of gods and goddesses before the worlds began.

She found a collective of elves, fae, and gnomes who had dedicated themselves to the songs of the stars and their union with land and sea. It was they who introduced her to prophecies of rebirth and return, and an ancient enemy who would negate all of these.

"You are dear to us," her collective of stargazers said from beneath the painted canopy of stone that served as the Underland sky, "but you must heed the call of the ones above. It is time you answered. In you, the story lives on."

With great sadness, the mermaid consented to their advice, and the siren in her heart leapt for joy between the waves. But before she could resume her studies and share what she had learned beneath the earth, there was one place to which her soul had to return.

She boarded a ship that bore her out over the southern seas, to the waters that had ripped her mother away so many years ago. The land and ocean were twisted, dark, howling with death and disease.

A haunting voice picked up over the water, warning of the dangers below. Her siren-heart paused to listen—*This is a song I know.* The mermaid took up the melody, calling upon the wind and waves to guide the ship to safe harbor, and the stars to watch over those who glided across the ocean and see them safely home. They answered the mermaid's song. The ship found its way back, and her sacred vow was renewed.

So long as she retold the stories of the stars and carried them in her heart across the world, the mermaid's siren magic ebbed and flowed. She carried on her parents' legacy, recording the tales and movements of the stars above and aiding those they smiled on across land and water below.

KATARINA

Katarina's throat thickened as she watched over Teodric while he slept. Her siren magic bound his wounds, restoring what had been broken the evening before.

"Hearts are not so easily mended," the sea witch liked to say, "in worlds above or worlds below." A truth she well knew.

The scholar rose and walked to the door of the young

man's chamber. His father stood just outside, wringing his hands.

"How is he?" Frederick moved to go inside, but she caught his arms.

"He is asleep, but he should be fully healed in a day or two."

The nobleman's brow knit. "But how—"

"The sea has great plans for your son, Lord Adhemar. Will you entrust her to keep her secrets for a time?"

Frederick peered over her shoulder, his own lowering as he saw the steady rise and fall of his son's chest. "These next few months will be hard on him." He led Katarina into their living quarters and motioned for one of the castle servants to bring them tea. Frederick's hands brushed through his hair, causing the dark brown with tendrils of gray to stand on end. "I thought it would break my heart to tell Aurelia that he had left, that I didn't know when we would see him again." Tears welled in his eyes. "But this . . ." His head fell.

Katarina knelt on the floor and took his hand. "You must trust your son to be strong. If it is meant to be, he will see Iellieth again." Incarnations of Lilia had taken other lovers over the millennia—she did not have to find Hugh, if he were even present on this plane.

"Have you traveled to Nortelon before?" Frederick squeezed her hand and settled back into his chair, taking up the tea and saucer.

She shook her head. "No, I cannot say that I have." Her mother had traveled far south of Nortelon, and its sea borders abutted those of Nepta, but she had never set foot in the port city herself, preferring Caldara when she was on land. "You and your family will be sorely missed, Lord Adhemar."

A small smile crossed his face. "If I can see joy on their faces again—the way my wife looked when she learned that we would be moving to this castle, the way my son's face lights up when he sees Iellieth—I'll know I didn't fail."

Wind whipped past the castle walls, a squall gathering in the deeps. The magic that flowed from her core shivered. Something waited on the horizon for this family. A rising shadow. "I hope you will come to see the truth even outside of that. But, Frederick . . ." One aspect of the midnight alarm and request for aid still eluded her. "How did you know to call me?"

The nobleman chuckled and shook his head. "Would you believe me if I said it was the whisper of the sea?"

CHAPTER 14

KATARINA

Katarina pursed her lips as she stepped back from Teodric's bedside. All morning, she had debated bringing him pages from Hugh and Lilia's story. He was sleeping when she arrived. Carefully, she'd laid her recent translations on his lap and crept away.

She believed in the power and possibility of stories, but in this case, would the tale be helpful? Would it give him what he needed?

When she was halfway to the door, Teodric called for her, head tilted and eyes heavy as he withdrew from what she hoped was a deep sleep. He thumbed through the pages, opening the bindings to the first to trail his fingers over the curled script of the title, *The Ballad of Hugh and Lilia*. "She told me a little about this story," he said softly. His gaze drifted to that far-off place where Iellieth lived in his memory. "She told me that it was a love story, but that it seemed like it would be a sad one."

Teodric lowered his head, and she waited for him to collect himself. His eyes shone bright as he looked up, hope and grief warring across his expression. "Do they end up together, Katarina?"

She sighed, smiling sadly. The young nobleman was looking for hope, but she could only offer him truth and uncertainty. "Not in that lifetime, no."

Teodric frowned. He didn't understand, not yet.

"Many stories are more complex, more varied than they at first appear." She kissed his forehead and withdrew to the door. "There are special tales, like this one, that must not only be retold, but relived, again and again." Her smile deepened, as she thought of the recurring Lilias through the ages, at times searching for Hugh, at times fulfilling other aspects of her greater purpose. "Those stories, they're the ones we haven't quite gotten right, at least not yet. But one day." She took a deep breath, the reassurance as much for Teodric as it was for herself. Knowing Iellieth —putting a smile, a face, a soul to the stories she loved— complicated the promise she'd found in the tales before they'd met. In this moment, the melancholy of Lilia's plight, her returning, weighed heavy on Katarina's heart. How many of the decisions that Iellieth made, that were made around her, were truly hers in isolation, and how many were already part of the war for the age, for Azuria?

Teodric cleared his throat and flipped past the first chapters. "But one day," he repeated. "Thank you, Katarina."

She bowed her head and slipped out of the room, leaving him to read and to rest.

LILIA

Lilia's heart pounded as she tore through the trees, sobs threatening to rend her chest in half. Their forest, their home were simply . . . gone.

Criane and the other seers had been right in their warnings, and yet what they foretold was too painful for the fae to hear. It was even more painful to experience.

When Lilia shut her eyes, the flames licking the base of the elder tree that had been her home filled her vision —the sacred oak that tied them to both this plane and the Brightlands, whose roots grew so deep that she held the forest in her sprawling limbs.

Within days of the arrival of Alessandra's forces, all that they held dear was wrenched away.

In the fighting, a poisoned arrow had struck her mother's side, a foul, creeping substance coating her skin. Lilia had guided Enid out of the clearing, calling desperately for Eravenor. The antlered doe appeared, whisking the reya to safety and leaving Lilia to oversee the retreat.

Two loss-filled days followed as they hid on the outskirts of their destroyed home. Smoke still curled up from the remains of the forest. With each breath, it coated their lungs.

"Breathe deeply, fae children," Criane had urged. "Let us not forget the fires of this day, the evil of the goddess who seeks only to obliterate and destroy." The elderly fae hacked horribly from the smoke hovering in her lungs. "There will be sunless days before the wars are done, and worse before the wars are won." Following a second fit of coughing, she lifted her hands. "But hear this—we inhale the spirits of the forest. We honor them in our bodies. And we take them on from here to our new realm."

Lilia's foggy breath caught in her chest. Surely she had misheard the seer's words.

She slipped through the healers gathered outside her mother's tent, kneeling down at Enid's side.

Enid took her daughter's hand, cupping it between her own. "Soon, my child, our people will look to you as their reya." The fae queen took a wheezing breath. The poison had seeped across her mother's skin. Its claws stretched over her neck, clutched tight about her throat in a choking black moss. "I formed you from the best parts of myself, Lilia."

The fae princess shook her head, striving to hold back the tide of her mother's words. "No, we can heal this. We can—"

"My child." Enid's breath gurgled in her throat. "The dark goddess comes to negate and to destroy. We cannot allow her dominion over the people of light." Her mother's eyes squeezed shut against the pain of the poison coursing through her. "If ever she were to gain a foothold over our magic, the worlds would be doomed."

Lilia pressed her lips tight together, tears streaming down her face. Her mother couldn't leave her, couldn't leave her people. Not like this.

Enid cried out, and the healers rushed to her side. Weakly, she pushed them away.

"When I die, child, I will return to stand beside Izadra." Her breath squeezed through the choking of the dark moss. Its tendrils crept past the graceful lines of her mother's chin toward her full lips. Enid's eyes drifted away as though she could already see the stars through the draped fabric overhead. "Still she misses Verdigris." The fae queen had been created when Verdigris, the Titan of Nature divided herself into three to form the planes of life

—those of shadow, brightness, and their balance. As she did so, the titan's spiritual body also split, forming her daughters Enid, Evelyn, and Lyric.

The fae queen exhaled slowly, her eyes fluttering shut as her head fell back upon her pillow. "Find my sisters or their daughters, Lilia." Three rapid breaths screeched into her lungs. Her mother shuddered, and Lilia held back a scream. "You must," Enid whispered. "Our people look to you to guide them to safety. Take care of them."

Enid's mouth fell slack, and a guttural cry broke free from the center of Lilia's being. The healers jumped back away from her, their arms half-extended to care for their fallen queen. Lilia crumpled onto the ground, pressing her body toward the earth that would never again share its energy with her mother. The roots rose to meet her, to wrap her in their grief. They erupted around the fae queen and entwined to cover her, flowers and bright green vines sprouting along their branches.

The earth roiled, undulating as ocean waves throughout the fae camp. The seers and the council took up Lilia's cry, their hearts yawning wide at the gap where Enid's presence, her light had once been.

Lilia knew nothing beyond the tremors of the earth until somehow, impossibly, Hugh was there, by her side. The nature spirits had called him. He lifted Lilia into his arms and held her tight against his chest.

Half her being had been ripped away by Alessandra's poison—first in the destruction of their home and now in the absence of her mother. She knew not who she was without their shared spirit.

Across the verdant earth, a dark spirit swarmed toward Lilia. The specter grinned wide. Protecting her people would mean separating from Hugh, putting this plane behind them, and returning to the Brightlands—where they belonged. Where she would be nothing but a shell of her former self.

⁂

"LILIA." HUGH'S WHISPER REACHED HER THROUGH THE undergrowth. She stopped, searching the trees for her lycan lover. They had only a few moments to share before she had to lead her people across the mountains and into the Brightlands. The weight of her responsibility for the fae hung heavy at the base of her throat. She had never wanted this. And yet the mantle was hers. Her mother's dying wish.

"Lilia." He called a second time. She found his voice amid a cluster of hawthorns. Lilia leapt between the trunks and into the glade of trees.

Immediately, Hugh's strong arms encircled her. He searched for her lips in the dim red fog, crushing his body to hers. Lilia gasped as the lycan's hold tightened around her waist. Hugh's beard scratched her cheek, her neck as his lips ventured down, following the pulse of her throat.

Opposing forces grasped either side of Lilia's heart. Her mother had warned her that Alessandra would stop at nothing to capture them and extract their magic. To survive, the seers were certain, they had to flee to the Brightlands. "We cannot protect you here, Reya," Criane had said to her. "The earth is too varied, the spirits weak." Lilia grimaced at hearing her mother's title applied to herself. "And be assured, it's you she's after."

Hugh's duty to his people similarly bound him. He couldn't deny Fenrir, the wolf god, and she couldn't abandon her people or condemn them to her mother's fate.

Grief rippled in the back of his throat as he tasted her skin. Lilia placed her hands on either side of his face and pulled away, waiting for his eyes to meet hers.

Eravenor had stood patiently by as she rehearsed what she had to tell him. The doe's reaction was more placid than she knew his would be. "Hugh," she whispered, "you must listen to me. There is a belief among my people that though we are separated, we find the ones we love again."

The lycan's jaw throbbed. He shook his head, not wanting to heed what she was desperate to say, the one hope she had to cling to.

Lilia's voice broke as she continued. "It may not be in this life or the next but—"

"No." The word emerged a hoarse groan. "We are meant to live *this* life as the only one that we have, Lilia. What if there's nothing left after this?" His sea-gray eyes burned against the lingering smoke around them.

Her lips trembled. "There has to be." Lilia's mouth twisted as Hugh turned away. He strode back, trying to rein in the grief surging between the two of them.

He stilled as he returned and ran soft fingers through her hair. "I will love you forever, with every part of my being."

"And I, you," Lilia answered.

Hugh was wrong about the ways of the gods. He had to be. For some souls, her mother had explained, a single lifetime was sufficient to accomplish their task. They traveled on from the planes of life and made their way to Astralei. But for others, a single lifetime wasn't enough. And those souls lingered on. They returned. Lilia held tight to her belief that one day, she and Hugh would find each other again. Their destinies would lead them closer together rather than farther apart. It had to be true. A tear fell from her eyes. Hugh caught it with his thumb and joined his lips gently to hers. Their tongues intertwined, sealing their promise to one another until that day when fate would draw their paths together again.

TEODRIC

In the week that followed the attempted escape and attack, Scad brought Teodric all the news he could. Guards remained stationed outside both entrances to Iellieth's room. The Hadvarian nobleman had stormed out of the castle sometime during the cloudy days Teodric was in and out of consciousness, incensed at his near-betrothed's rumored flight. Teodric did his best to calm his young friend, to assure him that Iellieth would be let out soon— probably after the duke forced Teodric and his family to leave under pretense of his father being made a diplomat to the coastal city of Nortelon across the Infinite Ocean.

He wrote to Iellieth every day, crumpling the letters in frustration rather than sneaking them off to Scad. What if harm befell Scad because of him? Or Iellieth were put in further danger? In the end, he scrawled a final, short note and entrusted it to Katarina, to pass off to Iellieth when the time was right.

I meant what I said to you. I'll return if ever I'm able and whisk you away.

Ever yours,
Teodric

He would write to her again from the ship that would carry them across the sea and from Nortelon, the vestiges of his hopes borne back over the waves that separated them.

Teodric held tight to his mother's shaking frame as they stepped aboard the *Fate & Favor*. The captain bowed his head and welcomed Teodric and his family aboard, guiding them to the stern and their quarters. "It's an honor to be escorting His Majesty's diplomats, my lord," he said, reaching out for his father's hand.

"And our honor to do the king's service." Frederick took the captain's hand firmly in his grasp before he escorted Mother into their quarters. "What a nice view you'll have, my love."

Teodric walked away to give them some privacy and stationed himself along the ship's railing, staring up at the castle high on the cliffs above.

"She's quite a sight, eh?" The captain approached and clapped him on the shoulder.

"Io Keep? Yes, sir, the—"

"She's the pinnacle we look for, sailing for weeks as we do. When she catches the sun's gleam, with the rest of the city shimmering below . . ." The captain shook his head. "Nothing like it, lad."

Teodric squinted up at the gray stone arches and the shining windows of the castle above, his gaze trailing over the parapets, bounding up until he reached Iellieth's window. Was she still there, trapped by her stepfather? Was she watching for him, sitting on her windowsill and searching the ships far below? His breath faltered at what he thought was a moving shadow behind her glass. He squinted harder. It might have been only a gull, a trick of the light, or his own wishful thinking.

He leaned his elbows back on the railing, staring up. If she could see him, she should know—what? That his mother's heart was broken, and her fragile nerves might never recover? That his father's career and their family's scant fortune were ruined? That whatever confidence or ease he pretended to possess couldn't span the living ache he felt at her absence? In the early spring, once the duke's agents had stopped searching for them, they would have sailed together, all the way to the Elven Realms. She could have attended their fabled school while he roamed the wilds. Or they could have traveled south and visited the ancient city of Andel-ce Hevra, taken in its wonders together.

All those dreams were gone now.

Through garbled yells and rapid movements, the crew freed the *Fate & Favor* from the docks to cross the Infinite Ocean. The way she'd smiled at him, the light in her eyes as they met in the hall—he knew what she hadn't had the chance to say. Once more, he felt the ghost of her hand torn from his grasp, their connection severed. The soldiers' fists. Iellieth dragged away.

A stone settled in the pit of his stomach, its ripples spiraling out across his entire being. As they calmed, a chilling truth remained. He would never see her again.

Teodric turned away from the gleaming castle and closed his eyes, left alone with the song of the sea.

ENDINGS ARE NOT ALWAYS WHAT THEY SEEM

Will Teodric be able to keep his promise to Iellieth and return? Will Iellieth ever find the life of adventure she longs for? Will Scad continue to be the best friend a half-elven noblewoman could ever ask for? (I will spoil that one —yes!)

Uncover the next phase of Iellieth and Teodric's journey in *Buried Heroes*, where their lives have taken unimaginable turns and a thrilling destiny awaits.

If you loved the magic and romance of *Song of Parting* and you're craving more adventure, your journey continues in *Buried Heroes*. Calderon's plots to force Iellieth into marriage continue, and Teodric's life upon the high seas unfolds in ways he could never have imagined.

The fate-bound magic of Hugh and Lilia continues to exert its pull over our heroes' stories. **Find more adventure, enchantment, and dangers galore in the first novel in the Age of Azuria high fantasy series.**

A RUNAWAY NOBLEWOMAN. A CURSED WARRIOR. AND THE QUEST TO SAVE THEIR WORLD.

Buried Heroes is an epic fantasy adventure filled with magic and destiny with a slow-burn romance subplot.

Step into a world of forgotten kingdoms, ancient relics, and a prophecy that will change everything. If you love found family, reluctant heroes, and forbidden magic, then continue your fantasy adventure with Buried Heroes!

CURIOUS ABOUT IELLIETH'S AMULET AND HOW IT FELL into her mother's possession? Hint: it involves a forbidden romance at the Amastacia family's seaside estate . . . Find out by visiting bethballbooks.com/aurora to join my newsletter and get a free copy of *Aurora*, the prequel novella for the *Age of Azuria* series!

The battle for an age begins more simply than one might think—an elven diplomat, a human noblewoman, and the forbidden love that would change their world, forever.

Elven diplomat Dorric Themear has experienced the giddy flutterings of new love before. But not like this. Behind the sapphire eyes of Lady Emelyee Amastacia lies a long-awaited destiny that neither of them can sense or stop.

However, forces darker than Emelyee's husband are prepared to stand in their way.

Close on the couple's heels, Ridel, one of Lucien's most trusted servants, is less than enthused about her assignment to watch the would-be lovers. If only her master had been visionary enough to see that a child cannot result if the parents are dead. She'll do her best to comply with his orders to observe and to wait—at least for now.

Although Dorric and Emelyee do not suspect the role they play in the larger story of Azuria, they have a secret protector lingering in the shadows, preparing for precisely this moment. High in the Frostmaw Mountains, Yvayne has seen the signs of the turning of the age before. This time, with the proper intervention, she and the druids can make their play for Azuria.

In this prequel novella for the *Age of Azuria* high fantasy series, competing forces converge in a battle for the future of their world—a future that hangs upon the return of a long-awaited soul. And, of course, on Dorric's ability to woo the human noblewoman whose affections lie beyond his reach.

Visit bethballbooks.com/aurora for a free copy of *Aurora*, the prequel novella for the *Age of Azuria* series, and find out where Iellieth's story truly began!

You'll find other exclusive stories as part of the Circle of Story, my newsletter community for all the latest book news and update. Visit the link above to join!

❧

OTHER TALES OF FIGHTING TO DETERMINE ONE'S FATE LIE AHEAD

Iellieth and Teodric are not the only two fighting against forces larger than themselves to decide their future. *For fans of stabby heroines and revenge quests, a prequel novella driven by danger, destiny, and sisterly affection.*

Unlike her sister Piper, who fantasized about Serrana's elegance while growing up in the forest, Natalya never saw romance in the city's stone walls. Their views on the life of a courtesan were similarly divided—Piper knew it was her destiny to attain such a distinguished role, while Natalya preferred the pursuit of other accomplishments, particularly those that could be earned at the end of a magical dagger.

Rising through the ranks of Serrana's most dangerous thieves' guild rather than those of society, she's gained a reputation throughout Serrana. Merchants and sailors alike fear the sneaking, moonlit shadow of "the Blade."

But when Piper's Suzerain faces financial ruin, threatening Piper's freedom, Natalya will stop at nothing to rescue her sister from the back-stabbing nobles of Serrana's court.

After all, rescuing sisters is precisely what blades are for.

It will take all of Natalya's cunning, her friendships, and the magical destiny she's denied to free Piper from her plight. And even that may not be enough.

Dive into the twisted wiles of Serrana's competing powers, rescue those you love, and swear your revenge in this prequel dark fantasy novella for the *Heir of Lilith* series.

A HIGH-STAKES FANTASY ADVENTURE
WHERE LOVE AND FATE INTERTWINE.

Song of Parting is only the beginning.

Iellieth and Teodric's adventures continue in _Buried Heroes_ where you'll find an immersive fantasy world filled with political intrigue, mythical creatures, and an unbreakable bond.

Keep reading for a sample from _Buried Heroes_ and where we rejoin Iellieth on her adventure!

IELLIETH

FIVE YEARS AFTER THE EVENTS OF SONG OF PARTING

Iellieth trailed her fingers lightly across the tall wildflowers trapped inside their designated plot in the castle gardens. She breathed in their shy, hopeful aromas as she passed. A memory trickled by from when she had been only as tall as they, running through the fields outside of Aurora, ready to show off her newest discovery. The flowers' faces seemed to turn toward her as she walked; they alone would bear witness to the tears that gathered in her eyes. She would be forced to leave them behind, like everything else that had grown in her years here. But however hopeless the situation appeared, she was determined to have a say in her ultimate destination.

She and Katarina had arranged to meet in her favorite spot in the gardens, just at the edge of the Arboretum. Many others had claimed it as a cherished location since Iellieth started tending it a few years before. She felt more at peace than she had in days as the blush-flowering trees poked their arms above the other greenery and beckoned her forward to their petaled embrace.

When she first told Mathilde, the gardener, what she wanted to plant in the formerly overgrown bed, the woman had scoffed. The Lady surely had her head in the clouds if she believed the spring-blossoming trees would grow beneath the shelter of the carefully groomed forest. They wouldn't receive enough sun, and if they did grow, they would cast too long a shadow over the collections of crimson and ivory flowers Iellieth wanted to cultivate beneath them.

"Breathtaking as always, Lady Amastacia." Katarina feigned a short curtsy from beneath the stone archway.

Iellieth grinned and hurried forward. "Did you catch sight of yourself in a mirror, or are you waxing poetic about the flowers?"

Katarina laughed at Iellieth's teasing. She extricated herself from the raptures of the climbing roses and embraced her friend. "How are you?" she asked as she leaned away to look at her face.

"I am as alright as you would guess." It seemed they were alone in the gardens, but the fresh growth obscured the far bends too fully to be sure.

"I cannot believe it's finally here."

"Nor can I."

"And there's no way they can be talked out of it?"

Iellieth sighed. "No, dear Katarina, not that I have found."

"Well, I find it truly abominable—"

"Wait, please. We cannot all be free-roaming Celestial scholars, and I would choose for . . ."—her voice grew husky as the tears gripped her throat once more—"for our final chat to be of something more high-minded than my stepfather's scheming. One last story, before I go." Katarina loved telling stories and would never be able to resist such a request, especially under the circumstances. "A new one."

Katarina grinned at her as a tear fell from her dark eyes and carved a path across her warm brown skin. "Very well." She pulled Iellieth's arm through her own, and they began their final walk together around the gardens.

"There was once a beautiful oread, one of the dryads of the mountains, who would disguise herself as a human and tell her tales to curious travelers making their way from one land to the next. Eramis, that was her name. What Eramis valued, as most oreads do, was a mingling between cultures so that all lands might be joined, especially through their stories, one to the other.

"The type of traveler Eramis encountered determined the story she told. Those who left their small villages seeking adventure learned of distant, exotic lands where even their wildest dreams for what life might contain would be surpassed. Those who returned home from a long journey heard of incredible transformations or revelations that others had experienced after an extended time alone on the road, engaging with the sanctity of the land around them.

"But Eramis's favorite story to tell was that of Hugh and Lilia, two great heroes of old. He was the leader of the lycan people, the first humans to emerge on the surface of the prime plane, protected by the wolf god Fenrir in their journey across the lands. One day as he ventured through the forest, he heard a heartbreakingly gorgeous song that danced its way between the trees to nuzzle against his ears.

"Oreads are beautiful mistresses of song, as you recall I'm sure, so this part of the story is somewhat suspect. It's possible that Eramis inserted herself in some ways into the role of Lilia in the romance, which is of course up to her to do as the storyteller, but it bears noting all the same.

"Hugh tore through the forest in search of the singer, sure that his life would be forever darker if he could not find the being behind the song. And there ahead of him, with her pale hand pressed against the firm body of an oak tree, was Lilia.

"She looked rather like you if the stories are to be believed. Deep red hair that cascaded all the way to her waist and mystical green eyes starred through with gold.

"The lycan alpha was caught off guard by the embodiment of loveliness before him, and he stopped, frozen in his tracks. Lilia's bright eyes turned slowly at the disturbance she felt in the woods. In the space of a heartbeat, she withdrew a deep green bow and notched an arrow. 'Who dares disturb our morning ritual, between the woods and I?' she demanded. Hugh stumbled back, surprised by the aggression from what he had previously seen as pristine beauty.

"By this point in the story, Eramis would have walked for some time with the traveler and would know which part of the legendary love between the two they might most need to hear. And, in that tradition, thinking of our friendship, I'll leave you with the end.

"A great tragedy overtook the world and drove apart what had previously been woven together by the natures of magic and time. Hugh and Lilia faced a choice: to abandon their peoples or to be divided from one another. They each chose the latter, though it was the hardest thing they'd ever done. He remained with the humans on the prime plane. She retreated with the other fae to the Brightlands, a realm of wild beauty and mischievous magic well suited to their empathetic, curious natures.

"Enid called the soul of her daughter into the heavens after a time, and Fenrir brought his warrior to a place of peace. Through the ages, they would long for one another, as we long for those we are separated from, either through space, time, death, or other machinations. Some believe that this longing proves that we are alive. Others, that it marks the path forward."

"What do you think it means?" Iellieth asked, knowing Katarina was fond of burying lessons inside ancient tales.

"I believe the answer is somewhere in between the two. Many emotions remind us of the life pulsing through our veins. Many forces conspire together to illuminate the roads ahead. We live, learn, and love by both."

"I shall dearly miss your stories, Katarina." Their moments together were among her few bright memories of life in the castle.

"And I shall dearly miss you, Iellieth. In my heart, I want to tell you that things may turn out better than they seem, but I don't wish to make your journey any heavier than it is already."

"Thank you." Iellieth turned to go before the parting became more difficult, but Katarina caught hold of her arm.

"Are you sure that telling your mother about Lord Stravinske's behavior would do nothing to change her mind?"

Iellieth shook her head and suppressed the shudder in the middle of her spine. "She and the duke know exactly what sort of man he is. Nothing of that sort could possibly be a surprise. I already tried to tell her before, and she did nothing."

"But he—"

"He may have his wedding ceremony, and a night or two at most if I can do nothing to prevent it. But I'll not endure longer than that. What the duke means to be a cage, I mean to be a step, however unwelcome, to freedom. I'll find someone who doesn't know who I am, book passage across the ocean, and make my way to the Realms."

"Are you hoping to seek out Teodric, after you find your father?"

"It has been years, Katarina. I haven't heard from him since we tried to escape, and his aid to me brought about the ruin of his family. He doesn't want to see me. I'm sure he has only painful memories of our past now."

"I wish there were more that I could do, Iellieth."

The sob she had struggled to hold back leapt from her chest, and Iellieth threw her arms around her friend. "You've given me access to worlds I could never have otherwise known, to languages and literatures extending beyond these lands and back through time. I would never have been able to endure all of this, to find a way to survive, without the tools you placed in my hands."

Katarina's tears mingled in her hair as she was sure her own were doing in her friend's twisted locks. *"Kev'rei mau, adeli lei,"* she whispered into Iellieth's neck. *I'll never forget you*, in the language of the Celestial realm, their favorite to translate together. Katarina kissed the pointed tip of Iellieth's ear and stepped back. "I'll be there to see you off at the Lyceum. Take care."

She squeezed Katarina's hand. "Until then." Iellieth turned toward the garden's side entrance. In a trick of the early morning light, the beds of flowers appeared brighter, more vivid than they had only a few minutes before.

Hadvar, where she and her family would transmigrate later that morning, was too far to the north to have open-air gardens. They kept them only in glass houses, trapped and forced to stare through panes to capture the life-giving rays of the sun.

*I*ELLIETH *AND* *T*EODRIC'S *ADVENTURES CONTINUE IN* Buried Heroes, *book one in the* Age of Azuria *epic fantasy series!*

ABOUT THE AUTHOR

Beth Ball is a weaver of words and worlds spinning stories of druidic magic and the power of nature that span the epic fantasy realms of Azuria and Eldura. If you enjoy lyrical tales of action and adventure, dragons, werewolves, fae, wily foxes, and more, then grab your enchanted amulet, flaming longsword, poisoned dagger, or other mystical accessory of choice, and let's start our adventure!

You can find more of Beth's work and the legends of Azuria and Eldura at bethballbooks.com. For signed copies and exclusive art prints, visit bethballbooks.shop.

GLOSSARY

WORLDS & PLANES

Planes of Life, *three interconnected planes,* Azuria, Shadowlands, and Brightlands
Elemental Planes, one for each element, ruled over by and encompassing the power of each elemental titan
Astralei, spirit plane
Eldura, the name for the world in Azuria's ancient past before the Great Flood

ELEMENTAL TITANS

Ignis, titan of fire
Atamos, titan of air

Ilona, titan of light
Gaia, titan of earth
Thalyssa, titan of water
Nyx, titan of darkness
Verdigris, titan of nature, *destroyed and transformed into the three planes of life*
Izadra, titan of space, *destroyed and transformed into the spirit plane, Astralei*

DEITIES

Alessandra, "the dark goddess," goddess of negation
Cassandra, goddess of fate, patron deity of the saudad
Ewan'il, guardian deity of hunters, forest spirit
Fenrir, god of wolves; creator of daimon and Lycan
Kleodna, goddess of the sea
Llewelyn, prime goddess of the Positive Planes (including the Planes of Life)
Pandora, prime goddess of the Negative Planes

FOLKLORIC HEROES

Hugh & Lilia, a Lycan and a fae, respectively; heroes before the Fall of the First Age who sacrificed their love to save their peoples
Daughters of Verdigris, Evelyn (creator of the lummenfae [Shadowlands fae], mother of Ravenna, and grandmother of Yvayne), Enid (creator of the brightfae [Brightlands fae] and mother of Lilia), and Lyric (creator of druids whose magic transferred to the prime plane)

HISTORICAL EVENTS

War of the Champions, world-defining war between the Cities United and Alessandra, occurs shortly before the Great Flood
Great Flood, rising waters worldwide that brought about the end of Eldura and, in the aftermath, saw the world reborn as Azuria

PEOPLES OF AZURIA

Champions, mortals chosen by the titans and blessed with elemental magic, heroes of the world of Eldura; deities can also appoint a champion or a Chosen who serves their will upon the Planes of Life
Daimon, great wolves or dire wolves, created by the god Fenrir who also created the Lycan
Druids, mages and those bound to the earth, live in conclaves
Lycan, werewolves who were the first humans upon the Planes of Life, the second people of the wolf god Fenrir
Saudad, storytellers and travelers blessed by the goddess Cassandra

www.ingramcontent.com/pod-product-compliance
Lightning Source LLC
Chambersburg PA
CBHW021737190726
48288CB00009B/3086